THE BOY FOR ME

JANE CLAYPOOL MINER

SCHOLASTIC INC.
New York Toronto London Auckland Sydney Tokyo

*With much love,
for my niece, Junie Claypool*

Cover Photo by Owen Brown

ISBN 0–590–32370–9

Copyright © 1983 by Jane Claypool Miner. All rights reserved. Published by Scholastic Book Services, a division of Scholastic Inc.

12 11 10 9 8 7 6 5 4 3 2 1   4   3 4 5 6/8

THE BOY FOR ME

A Wildfire Book

WILDFIRE TITLES
FROM SCHOLASTIC

One

Maggie Matthews lay on the hand-knotted Swedish rug in front of the brick fireplace. One hand propped up her chin as she turned the pages of her *Sweet Sixteen* magazine with the other. Once in a while, she sighed and flipped over a couple of pages in slow boredom. She wasn't interested in the magazine, and she wasn't really looking at it.

The magazine was an excuse to be on the floor in front of the fireplace, because that was exactly where she needed to be. That particular spot was perfect because it was close to her brother Bob's bedroom. Her brother and his best friend, Tony Angelo, were in that room, and Maggie was eavesdropping.

She couldn't really hear much — just enough to figure out that they were talking about cars again. Once in a while, she could make out a word like "Chevrolet" or "transmission." Maggie couldn't help laughing at herself for eavesdropping so avidly on such a dull conversation. She knew she was being silly, but she couldn't help it. Anything and everything about Tony Angelo fascinated her these days. She was hopelessly in love with her brother's best friend.

As she turned the pages and eavesdropped, she reviewed her situation, telling herself that there must be some way out of this ridiculous obsession. How long had she been in love with Tony? Almost a year. And did he know it? Of course not. He didn't even know she was alive. Did she have any hope of ever getting him to notice her? Absolutely none.

She sighed again and sat up, then flopped out flat on the floor as if she were a rag doll. That's what she felt like — a spineless, cotton-stuffed, childish . . .

Bob and Tony burst out of Bob's room, crossing the living room to get to the kitchen. Each of them went to some trouble to jump over Maggie's limp body.

Maggie complained, "Can't you walk around me?"

Tony laughed and jumped backward, bridging her stretched-out legs one more time.

Though she knew he was just teasing, Maggie was delighted at any notice from Tony at all. She longed to find the words to hold him there even a few minutes longer. She wished with all her heart that she was the sort of girl who could flirt. But whenever Tony was around, she managed only to grumble or complain. Now, she tried to keep her voice light as she said, "You might trip."

2

Tony looked down at her and laughed at the thought. "I never trip," he declared easily. "How you doing, little sister?"

"I am not your little sister!" Maggie said in a voice that was almost a shout.

Tony's friendly face looked momentarily bewildered. Then he declared, "Good thing, too. You're too grouchy for me."

"You going to lie on the floor all day?" Bob asked. "Seems like that's all you've done all summer, Maggie."

"It's my summer," Maggie snapped at her brother. "I'll do whatever I want with it."

"Okay," Bob said and held up his hands to fend off imaginary blows. "Sorry I said anything. Good-bye, grouch."

Tony and Bob walked quickly from the room. Maggie sat up, drew her long legs up to her chin, and hugged herself close as she whispered, "Oh, Tony, can't you see why I don't want you to think of me as your sister? Tony, what can I do to make you really see me?"

Maggie tossed the magazine into the basket beside the fireplace, jumped up, stretched her arms over her head, and did twelve knee-bends in rapid succession. Then she opened her mouth and screamed with mock frustration.

Just then her cat, Ruffles, jumped on her back. Her mock scream turned into one of real pain. Maggie unhooked the cat's claws from her shoulder and held the cat up to her face. "You're a bad cat, Ruffles. You're not supposed to jump on me like that. Bad, bad cat." Then she shook the cat gently and smoothed down its soft fur. She pulled Ruffles close to her face so that the cat's whiskers tickled her cheek. She whispered, "I know why you're bad, Ruffles. You're bored. So am I. It's terrible to be sixteen years old. But it must be worse to be a cat and do the same things every day. How do you stand it, Ruffles?"

Ruffles batted one paw softly against her cheek in reply. Maggie laughed. Then her face fell into sadness. She whispered, "Oh, Ruffles, if only I could get Tony to understand that I'm grown-up now."

The ginger cat jumped from her arms and ran toward the kitchen. Maggie stretched her arms overhead and murmured to herself, "Maybe I should go outside for a while, too." It was almost the last week of summer vacation. They would all be cooped up inside a dull, musty classroom soon. She knew that staying inside on such a warm, glorious day was foolish. Nevertheless, Maggie picked up her magazine and went over to the couch. She sat down and began thumbing through the pages until she came to the article entitled "What Do Boys Want?" To no one, she said aloud, "I don't care what boys want. I care what *I* want. Me — Maggie Matthews."

She beat her chest with her fists, as though she were the lead in an old *Tarzan* movie. Then, she started to read. But she was quickly discouraged when she read that most boys wanted girls who were actively interested in the same things they were. That was more depressing news!

Tony was interested in cars and in reading *Playboy* magazine. She'd long ago decided that cars were not for her, and as for the magazine, that was too depressing even to think about. Despite her pessimistic thoughts, she went on reading. Maybe Tony would come in again, and she'd be here.

That made her think of the old movie she'd seen on television last night. That Olivia de Haviland certainly knew how to wait. Maggie began to imagine herself as a young woman who was kissing her boyfriend good-bye. It was World War I and her boyfriend, who looked exactly like Tony Angelo, was going off to be a fighter pilot. No! That wasn't a good daydream. The soldier in the movie was shot down, and Maggie certainly didn't want anything like that to happen to Tony.

She went back to the article, which said that boys liked girls with good personalities who were fun to be with. More bad news!

She wasn't always fun to be with, and she knew it. What was worse, Tony knew it. That was the trouble with falling in love with your brother's best friend. You were too familiar to have a chance. And yet, Maggie knew that Tony had been just familiar to her until that magical day a year ago.

It had been a warm summer day like this one. They'd been in the kitchen, making doughnuts for a party. Maggie could remember exactly how it had been. One minute Tony had been plain old Tony, and the next minute he'd been Prince Charming.

5

Not that Tony Angelo had ever been a frog or anything. He'd always been one of her favorite people. But that day, sometime between stirring the batter and popping the first doughnut into the electric fryer, everything had changed. She'd looked up, been dazzled by his bright smile, fallen deep into his warm, brown eyes, and almost fainted in surprise.

At first, she'd been so overwhelmed by her feelings that she'd followed Tony around like a little puppy dog. But Bob and he obviously thought of her as a pest, so she'd stopped that. This summer, her only thought had been to make Tony see how grown-up she was. Of course, it hadn't worked. Nothing worked, Maggie told herself sadly. Tony ate dinner at their house at least once or twice a week. As far as Tony was concerned, she was just Maggie — the tagalong. The only time he seemed to notice her was when she was a grouch.

As far as Maggie could remember, the last time that Tony had spoken directly to her — other than saying, "Pass the salt" — had been two weeks ago. That afternoon, he had looked up from his car magazine and his eyes had traveled slowly up the length of Maggie's long legs. Maggie felt herself blush at Tony's obvious interest in her. Was he finally going to notice how much she had changed? Was he finally going to see her as something other than Bob's kid sister?

She was wearing her white shorts and a bright red T-shirt.

Tony asked softly, "Mind if I ask you a personal question?"

"Of course not," Maggie answered as calmly as she could. Was Tony actually going to ask her a personal question in front of her brother Bob? At best, she had hoped that his obvious notice of her long, slender legs indicated that at some other, more private time . . .

Before her thoughts could go any farther, Tony asked, "Have you ever thought of trying out for the track team?"

"No!" Maggie snapped.

He said softly, "Your legs are so long, I think you might be able to run. I know you're tired of baseball. But with legs like those, you should be a runner. Why don't you try out for the team next spring?"

Maggie's hopes were dashed once again. Didn't he see her legs as *legs*? Didn't he realize how shapely they had become? She thought that when she dropped off the Babe Ruth baseball team last year she'd squelched her brother's and Tony's hopes that she would become a star athlete.

As she thought, Maggie frowned at the pictures of the beautiful girls in her magazine. There really wasn't much point in reading the stuff in magazines, she thought. Obviously, nothing was going to work with Tony.

She closed her eyes for a moment and thought about the summer day outside. She could almost smell the lake. She could almost hear the kids splashing in the water and the birds calling overhead. Why was she being such a ninny? Why didn't she go upstairs, get her swimsuit, and go out to the lake where the rest of the kids would be?

Even as she asked herself those questions, she knew the answer. Tony and Bob would be coming back soon. If she was lucky, they would stop and talk with her for a few minutes. Perhaps she would be able to share a sandwich and a Coke with them. At the thought of food, Maggie's stomach growled, and she remembered that she hadn't had anything to eat for hours.

Ignoring her stomach's complaints, she closed her eyes to see if her trick still worked. Sure enough, Tony's face appeared on the back of her eyelids. That had started happening right after the day in the kitchen. Now, she could see Tony's dark brown, curly hair, which was cut in a soft, round frame for his face. She could see the way it curled slightly over his ears. His merry, brown eyes were twinkling with fun. Tony had one of those wonderful faces that always seemed to be bursting with energy. He was alive with the excitement of living. She could see Tony's wide cheekbones and laughing mouth. She could almost hear him calling to her with his teasing voice, calling, "Hey, Maggie. Hey, little sister."

She opened her eyes and looked in the doorway. Sure enough, Tony had been calling her. It had not been a dream. Tony repeated his words, "Hey, little sister. Want some lunch?"

Maggie sat up straight and said in her most

sophisticated voice, "I've asked you not to call me 'little sister.' I'm not your sister."

Tony's face clouded for a moment. She could see she had hurt him, and that made her feel worse than ever. Nevertheless, she had to get him to understand that she was *not his sister* so she could get him to notice her as a person.

He laughed lightly as he said, "All right, Margaret Ann Matthews. Now, perhaps you will consider joining us for lunch?"

Maggie stood up, smiled, and walked quickly into the kitchen. She was happy she'd chosen to hang around the house today. Her gamble was paying off. Now she would have a few precious moments with Tony at lunch.

They worked together making the tuna salad sandwiches on wheat bread and the bologna-and-cheese sandwiches on rye. The boys talked lightly about their hobby of fixing up old junk cars and selling them. For over two years, Bob and Tony had been making quite a bit of money on restoring old cars.

Maggie was proud of them, because not many teenage boys were as capable and as intelligent as they were. At the same time, she envied them their lucrative hobby. Earlier, they had tried to teach her something about car mechanics. But Maggie knew mechanics would never be for her. She really didn't like machines. Though she had a working relationship with the computer in school and she drove her father's and mother's cars, she just wasn't very interested. It might have been nice, she told herself. Maybe it could have been a shared interest for Tony and her. But it was too late to start pretending now. Tony was no fool.

She put sandwiches on the table while Bob poured the milk and Tony raided the refrigerator for fruit and interesting leftovers.

As they sat down, Tony asked, "Not going out to the lake today?"

"No," Maggie said.

"I should think you'd want to go as much as you can. School starts in ten days," he said gently.

"Oh, those kids are so boring," Maggie answered. "They all seem so young to me."

If she had expected agreement or interest in her criticism of her friends, she was disappointed. Neither Bob nor Tony made any response to her remark. Instead, they continued their conversation about the 1968 Thunderbird that they were considering buying.

Maggie listened for a few minutes and then she said, "You know if you bring a third junk car into the garage, Dad will have a fit."

Bob shrugged his shoulders as though to say that it really wouldn't matter. Tony said, "She's right, Bob. And you know my folks won't let us leave it at our house."

Tony's parents didn't encourage him in his hobby at all. When Maggie was dreaming about Tony, she sometimes thought of him as a person who had had an isolated and tormented childhood.

It seemed rather romantic to think of Tony living in that big, old house with a mother and father who were as old as her own grandparents. She liked to think of Tony as an only child, though she knew that he had two brothers who were only ten years older. But when she was actually facing Tony Angelo across the kitchen table, it was very difficult to think of him as a dark and tormented person. His face was so sunny and open and warm. She had to admit that he was not a romantic hero out of a gothic novel. Instead, he was a very nice young man who just happened to be her brother's best friend.

Lunch finished, Bob turned to her and said, "If you do the dishes for lunch, I'll do them at dinner."

"It's your turn at dinner anyway," Maggie started. Then she relented and said, "Oh, never mind. I haven't got anything else to do anyway."

"Thanks a lot, kid," Tony said and gave her one of his flashing smiles.

When he smiled at her in that way, with his warm, brown eyes looking like the centers of the black-eyed Susans that grew in the empty field across the street, Maggie realized she would have done much more for Tony than wash the dishes. She felt her stomach tie into a knot. Her voice tightened as she said as casually as she could, "Are you guys going to be working in the garage this afternoon?"

Tony shook his head and said, "For about half an hour. Bob and I are going to the lake. Too bad you don't want to come along."

Maggie's heart sank. It would be fun to ride to the lake with Tony, even though she would be expected to join her own friends once she got there. Nevertheless, she didn't change her mind. Since her most important goal was to seem as grown-up and sophisticated as she possibly could, she didn't dare tell Tony and Bob she wanted to go now. They would see it as evidence of her childishness.

She felt sorry for herself as she watched the two boys drive away. There were almost tears in her eyes as she stood at the kitchen sink window looking out at the bright, green day. Her attempts to act sophisticated had painted her into a corner. Now there was nothing to do but stay home and read or watch TV.

She went to the bookcase and looked through a volume of romantic poetry. Much as she loved Tony, she admitted to herself she really wasn't in the mood for that. Finally, she went back to *Sweet Sixteen*.

She thumbed through until she found the section called "Natural Beauty Tips." There, she read with interest about the benefits of exercise. After reading the article, she looked in the mirror, checking her own golden-brown skin and light brown hair for indications of the various ailments that the article said lack of physical activity would induce. Her skin and hair seemed healthy enough even though she knew she wasn't getting as much exercise as she used to. Perhaps, since there was nothing else to do this afternoon, she could begin a beauty regimen. Maybe that would make her attractive enough to interest Tony.

Most of the hints corrected problems that she simply didn't have. The article told how to paint the tip of your chin with lighter makeup to correct a receding chin. Her own chin, though, was quite pointed and far from receding. Many of the other beauty hints attacked problems like curly hair or oily skin. Maggie knew she didn't have any of the problems that the magazine wanted to fix. What's more, she had none of the ingredients recommended for beauty treatments except mayonnaise and cucumbers — they were recommended as a natural remedy for dry skin. There wasn't really anything wrong with her skin, but she went to the kitchen and checked the cucumber supply anyway. There was only one cucumber, and her brother Bruce would need that for the salad tonight. It was his turn to cook. Nevertheless, she took the mayonnaise out and went back into the bathroom where she slathered it all over her face, rubbing it into her skin and hair.

She then went into the living room and put on a Police record. She began trying to follow the series of aerobic dances that were illustrated on page 75 of the magazine. It was a warm day so she soon worked up a sweat, and it felt good to move her body to the music. She was dancing just as fast as she could, lifting her legs high in the air, kicking fiercely as suggested in the "Aerobics for Beauty" article. She was actually having a good time.

It was so much fun that she wasn't as alert as she usually would have been. She didn't hear the kitchen door open. Tony was inside the living room and standing beside her before she noticed him. She was lifting her leg in the air, clapping her hands under her right leg, counting, "One-two. One-two." Then she switched to the left, lifting her left leg in the air, and counted, "One-two. One-two."

Behind her, she heard Tony's voice counting, "One-two. One-two."

Maggie stopped, whirled around, and screeched, "Tony Angelo, get out of here!"

Tony laughed. "But I was having fun."

"What are you doing here?" Maggie asked in the same voice.

"I came for our snorkel equipment. What have you got on your hair?"

Maggie's hand flew involuntarily to her mayonnaise-covered hair. She screamed at him, "Can't I have any privacy?" and ran from the room.

She ran to the bathroom and locked the door. She immediately turned on the shower to cover the sound of her sobs and she ran the water until she heard Tony pound on the bathroom door, calling to her, "Hey, Maggie. I'm sorry! Hey, come on out. Come on out!"

Tony pounded on the door a long time. When he stopped, she peeked out the small bathroom window, being careful not to get mayonnaise on her mother's white organdy curtain. She watched

14

Tony walk slowly back to his car and drive away. He didn't have the snorkel.

Maggie turned and looked at herself in the mirror. She saw that her face was red from crying. The greasy mayonnaise on her hair seemed to have whipped itself into a zoo of pointed snakes. More mayonnaise mixed with sweat ran down her red face, and onto the collar of her T-shirt. She said to her reflection, "I'll never speak to Tony Angelo again as long as I live. I'll never dare to!"

Two

Maggie was so humiliated by what she came to think of as the mayonnaise mess that she avoided Tony for the next two weeks. In fact, whenever she heard his car pull into the gravel driveway, she would make some excuse and go to her room.

It was painful — but not as painful as facing him. On the one night he stayed for supper, she was careful not to look directly at him. It was almost the same as not being there. But when school started on September 12, there really wasn't any way to avoid him. She had always ridden to school with Bob and Tony and her older brother Bruce.

This year, Bruce was going to be in college, but she would still be expected to ride with Tony and Bob. As she dressed for school that first day, she tried to look as grown-up as she possibly could. She was sixteen now, and a sophomore. That was a lot different from the silly little freshman she'd

16

been last year. This year, she promised herself, things would be different.

One of the promises she made herself that morning was that she wouldn't let Tony and Bob treat her as though she were an infant. After all, she was only eighteen months younger than Tony and nineteen months younger than Bob. It wasn't fair that she was two years behind them in school when she was really only a year and a few months younger.

Maggie wore her new white blouse with the lace on the collar and her best Levis. She hoped that the white blouse would indicate to Tony that she was ready to assume a more adult place in his life. Last year, she'd worn her old red T-shirt on the first day. Because last year, she'd hoped to convince Tony that she was too sophisticated to worry about dressing up. It hadn't worked. Maybe white lace would be a better way.

Tony's first words to her were, "Hi, kid. I hardly recognized you with clean hair."

Maggie's face flushed and she wanted to run and hide, though she knew that was impossible. She decided the best thing to do was brave it out. Instead of replying to his obvious reference to the mayonnaise mess, she ignored him.

But that didn't bother Tony. In fact, she was pretty sure he didn't even know he was being ignored. He and Bob talked happily all the way to school and Maggie sat in the backseat of the car, staring out at the green and bronze maple trees. She wished she were seventeen at least. Or that she had blonde hair. . . .

Her thoughts drifted off to the world of "if only . . ." The next thing she knew, she was standing on the steps in front of Hudson High. Tony and Bob were driving away to put the car in the senior parking lot.

Maggie looked up at the front doors of Hudson High and hugged her new pocketbook to her chest. She wished with all her might that this year might be different. "Oh, Tony," she whispered to the wind, "if you'd just look at me. . . ."

A friend called down to her, and she climbed the stairs. Soon she was busy talking about her summer. The first day started off well, and she didn't have time to think much more about Tony. Some of the kids she talked with thought she'd been away most of the summer because she hadn't been at the lake much. She smiled and looked vague, hoping to seem mysterious as she said, "I was so busy."

It was a good day and a good beginning. At least, everything went well until fifth period gym class. When she walked into the gym, Tony was standing in the middle of the gym floor, looking up at the basketball hoop. He was so darling that Maggie's first reaction was to smile in pleasure at seeing him.

He called out to her, "Hey, Maggie, over here." Clearly, he expected her to walk out to the middle of the gym floor and start talking to him as though they were good friends or something. Maggie realized that he didn't have a clue that she'd been snubbing him in the car that morning. As far as

Tony was concerned, everything was just fine, which only went to prove how little attention he paid to her.

There was nothing to do but walk to the center of the gym. She asked, "You going to be in this class?"

"Only temporarily," Tony answered. "Coach will get me a transfer next week."

"You should be in athlete's gym — sixth period," Maggie said.

"I will be," Tony answered. "My counselor thought that I should take advanced English. The coach is going to fix it."

"That's good," Maggie said.

Tony's eyes twinkled, and he teased lightly, "What's the matter? You don't want to be in the same gym class with me? Afraid I'll whip you at volleyball?"

"If you couldn't whip me at volleyball," Maggie said, "you'd be in pretty bad shape."

Tony's voice assumed that older-brother tone that he sometimes used with Maggie, and he said, "You really should try to be more athletic, Mag. You've got the body for it." Again, his eyes traveled over her long, lean, healthy body and he said, "You could amount to something if you tried, and you've got two years ahead of you."

Bob and Tony both ran track and played baseball. Her older brother Bruce had also been a baseball player. Maggie had once been the star of her Babe Ruth team, but she'd dropped out when she went to high school. The boys seemed to think it was a great tragedy. Bob, Bruce, and Tony all pointed out constantly that she had potential but that she lacked motivation.

Maggie shrugged her shoulders and shook her head as she said to Tony, "I'm just not interested. I never have been."

"I know," Tony answered, "but I'm just saying you could be. You could be crackerjack on the track team, Mag. I know you could."

Before Maggie had time to think of anything smart to reply, she saw Denise Meredith walking toward them. She rolled her eyes and said to Tony, "Here comes drippy Denise."

Tony laughed and shook his head as he chided, "Maggie, you really ought to try to get over that jealousy."

"Jealousy?" Maggie began. "I'd never be jealous of her!"

She wanted to explain exactly why she would never be jealous of her, but Denise was approaching hearing distance. Before Maggie really understood what happened, Denise was standing beside Tony with her arm intertwined in his, looking up at him with big, blue eyes. Her dark eyelashes seemed to be moving with the ferocity of a giant bat flapping its way out of a dark cave into the night sky.

"Oh, Tony," Denise said. "It's so great to see you. I wanted to ask you a question." As she talked to Tony she moved her body slightly, maneuvering it in such a way that her back was turned to Maggie. Maggie was suddenly outside looking in.

Maggie stood looking down at Denise's soft, red hair. She thought seriously about pulling handfuls of it out of the girl's head. If there was one person in the whole world that she absolutely could not stand, it was Denise Meredith. Everything about Denise annoyed her. She was annoyed by the way Denise's big, blue eyes and dark eyelashes seemed to shimmer with dramatic intensity over anything Tony said. She was annoyed by Denise's petite, darling figure and her kelly-green cheerleader outfit; and by Denise's long, red fingernails and the small, gold chains that circled her slim wrists. Above all, she was annoyed by the way Tony Angelo was looking down at Denise with such rapt attention. *For all he knows*, Maggie thought, *I might have been swallowed by a giant whale or have melted into a puddle of pink Jell-O and slithered across the gym floor.*

Maggie stood with her hands hanging at her sides, listening to the conversation between Denise and Tony. She would have liked to go away but she didn't seem to have any motor power. *Perhaps*, she thought, *jealousy has frozen me.*

As she stood on the outskirts of Denise and Tony's tidy little circle, she felt as though there ought to be something she could do or say to make Tony look at her the way he was looking at Denise. She wanted to jump up and down and shout. She wanted to throw her arms around Tony and talk to him with a silky voice. Somehow she should be able to drag his attention away from Denise and back to her. And at the same time, she was powerless over Tony Angelo. There was nothing that she could do except wait for another day.

She raised one hand in a halfhearted salute, then said, "Well, see you," as she turned to walk away.

Neither Tony nor Denise seemed to notice that she was leaving. That didn't surprise her because neither of them had seemed to notice that she was there.

She walked back to the gym locker room as quickly as she could. Maybe later when he came to her house there would be some way that she could capture his attention. Right now, at least, she was no competition for Denise.

But things were no different — and no better — that afternoon. Tony barely seemed to notice that she was alive. She was sitting watching an old movie on TV when he walked in the front door. He spoke to her mother and her older brother Bruce, asking, "Is Bob around?" but didn't even seem to notice Maggie at all.

Maggie spoke up quickly, saying, "Bob's in the garage. Shall I show you the way?" It was a stupid thing to say, of course, since Tony would be able to find his way to the garage blindfolded on a dark and stormy night. Nevertheless, Maggie wanted desperately to have some excuse to walk with Tony.

Tony looked at her with a mildly amused expression to see if she was joking and finally said in a soft drawl, "Sure, kid. You could use the exercise."

Maggie flushed at the reference to her sedentary ways and jumped out of the chair. As they walked out of the living room, through the hallway, and into the kitchen, Tony said yet again, "Maggie, you really should do something with that terrific body of yours besides sit in a chair. Do you want to grow up to be a soft slob?"

Maggie wanted to point out that Denise was even less athletic than she was. Instead, she asked, "How about if we go for a bike ride this Saturday? It would be good for me."

Tony nodded his head and answered, "It would be good for you, but Bob and I are going to go to a car auction in New Hope, so we won't be able to ride on Saturday."

Maggie waited for Tony to suggest a different day for the bike ride, but he didn't. Not wanting to be a pest, Maggie walked silently beside Tony.

Once inside the garage, she wondered why she was there. Tony and Bob immediately fell into a deep conversation about the cars. Maggie sat on a high, old stool in a corner, watching the two young men work on their latest acquisition. Tony and Bob were taking apart the carburetor of a 1973 Mercury and cleaning each individual part before they began trying to put the car into working condition.

As she watched the two boys work, she wished that she could turn herself into rusty, old metal.

If she were to have nuts and bolts for kneecaps and a broken wire for a spinal column and soft, fuzzy upholstery for skin, she knew that Tony would pay attention to her. As she sat on the high stool, she began making soft, purring motor noises under her breath.

Bob looked up and frowned and said, "Maggie, if you can't keep quiet, go inside."

Maggie, furious, jumped off the tall stool and went back into the house. It did absolutely no good to try to hang around those two when they were thinking about cars. There was no way in the world that she was going to get Tony to notice her in that garage. Not only was she no competition for Denise Meredith, she wasn't even competition for a broken-down 1973 Mercury!

Maggie spent the rest of the evening playing chess with her older brother Bruce as she listened for Tony and Bob to come back into the house. Often when they finished a work session in the garage, they would come back into the kitchen for a late-night snack.

The big, old farm kitchen of the Matthewses' house was really the center of activities. The boys and Maggie had always preferred to sit at the round, claw-footed oak table when they did their homework or played games. They claimed the light from the round, Victorian leaded-glass shade was brighter than the modern fixtures in other parts of the house. Her mother said they really liked the kitchen because it was close to the refrigerator. But Maggie loved the warm wood paneling and sparkling white cabinets. She always felt safe and happy in the kitchen. It was the best place to relax and be herself.

Though Maggie waited until ten o'clock that evening, neither Bob nor Tony came in. Finally, she heard Tony's car drive off, and Bob came into the house alone. He looked happy and satisfied as he poured himself a glass of milk and sat down at the kitchen table.

Maggie looked up from her chess game with her brother Bruce and said, "I'll never understand what you two find so fascinating about those beat-up old automobiles."

Bob just looked at her, grinned, and answered, "Maggie, I think you've got a motor block about automobiles. Don't you want to grow up to be a liberated woman? You need independence these days."

Maggie sniffed and said quickly, "I'm independent enough. There's more to liberation than cars, you know."

Bruce looked up and warned, "Watch your game, Maggie. Your queen's going."

Maggie looked back down at the chessboard and realized that, indeed, her queen was in jeopardy. For the next twenty minutes she had to pay extremely close attention to her chess game. Even so, her brother Bruce beat her. Though Bruce was a year older than Bob and going to college in a week, Maggie could usually beat him at chess. She had a natural talent for all mathematical and reasoning games. Bruce's talent was in art, and Bob was best at mechanics. At chess, though, Maggie could usually beat the rest of the family, but this time, when the game was over, she was the loser.

Maggie stood up, stretched, reached her hands to the ceiling, did some quick knee-bends, and said, "I'm tired. I think I'll go to bed."

Bob, who had been reading a car magazine while he drank milk and ate chocolate chip cookies, looked up and said, "I don't know how you get tired. You didn't do anything again today."

Maggie turned around, put her hands on her hips, and raised her voice in defense of herself. She said, "Listen, Bob, just because you're a year and a half older than I am doesn't give you license to pretend that you're my father. I'm leading a perfectly normal life for a sixteen-year-old girl, and I don't need your advice or criticism. Get that?"

Bob grinned and nodded his head as he replied with a swift salute, "Got it, Sergeant Margaret, and you're right, it's your life. If you want to turn into one of those drippy types who can't do anything, you go right ahead and behave the way you're behaving."

Maggie was angry as she retorted, "You don't have any idea what it's like to be me, Bob! So you don't have any idea how I should be leading my life. It's my choice. Maybe I'm improving my mind."

"Yeah, you may think so," Bob said, "but I don't think the magazines you're reading or the old movies you watch are exactly mind-improving. What I think is that you're ignoring your natural talents in order to fit in with the rest of the girls."

Maggie recognized that her brother was speaking out of real concern. She dropped her anger long enough to say, "I don't have anyone to do anything with anymore. I asked Tony to go on a bike ride this Saturday, and he said you guys were going to New Hope. Most of my friends are a lot less active than I am, you know."

Bob nodded his head in quick agreement. "I know. But you ought to look for some other friends. Judy Wilson is nice. How about seeing if she'd go on a bike ride?"

"Judy Wilson?" Maggie repeated incredulously. "She's not in my crowd."

"No. But she's a nice girl," Bob said. "She's smart, too."

"Yeah," Maggie replied. "She's smart and she likes old cars. Why don't you ask her out if you're interested in her? Don't try to palm her off on me."

Bob looked rather startled at the suggestion and then said, "Maybe I will. I never thought of it, but maybe I will. We could double-date with Tony and Denise on Saturday night."

Until then, Maggie hadn't been too concerned about the mildly serious conversation she and Bob were having. Now, her mood dropped into desperation. She felt a kind of churning in the pit of her stomach. She wondered if she might actually be physically ill. She asked, "Tony's taking Denise out Saturday night?"

Bob nodded. "Yeah, they're going to see a movie together. He wondered if I wanted to ask a date and go along." Then Bob seemed to sense some of her upset, because he asked, "You want to be my date, Maggie? I could take you to the movie Saturday night."

Horrified at the thought of going to the movies with her brother while Tony was out with someone else, Maggie rejected the possibility quickly. She turned to leave the room. Bruce, who had been putting away the dishes while she argued with Bob, asked, "Are you all right? Not sick?"

"I'm fine," she answered.

Maggie went to her room, flopped down on her bed, stared up at the yellow and red and green flowers on her wallpapered ceiling, and fought back the tears that were squeezing out of the corners of her eyes. She asked herself whether Denise and Tony's date meant what she was afraid it meant. Was Tony really interested in Denise? *Well, of course he is, dummy*, she told herself. After all, Tony Angelo had never asked *her* to go anywhere.

Let Tony Angelo date anyone he wants to, she told herself. She wasn't going to cry over some guy with dumb taste like that. If he didn't know any better than to take Denise Meredith out on a date, then he wasn't the boy for her. No, she was going to get over Tony Angelo if it was the last thing she did.

With that firm resolution, Maggie relaxed and let the tears slide down her face. She would get over him tomorrow. Tonight she was just too sad.

Three

Maggie spent the next weekend feeling sorry for herself and making up wild and impractical plans for getting Tony to notice her. She thought about farfetched things such as dressing up in an American flag or wearing all pink for two weeks in a row. She even considered writing him an anonymous letter in which she extolled her own virtues.

As she ran through all of the possible ways to get Tony Angelo to notice her, she became more and more convinced that it was hopeless. In the first place, what would Tony want with a girl like her when he seemed to be attracted to girls like Denise Meredith? At the thought of Denise, Maggie flopped over on her bed and stared at her wallpapered ceiling. Why had she fallen in love with her brother's best friend? Why couldn't she have picked some nice, attainable boy like Charlie Jones? Charlie was always asking her if he could help her with her math homework. For that matter, why did she have to be interested in boys at all? She had spent the first fifteen years of her life perfectly happy. Her important pursuits were bicycling, playing baseball, skateboarding, and ice skating. Now it seemed to her that for the last year all she'd done was lie around and watch old movies and think about Tony. She was getting tired of it.

In fact, she was getting so tired of it that she gave herself a deadline. She promised herself she would find some way to make Tony pay attention to her within the next month or she would give him up forever. At the thought of giving up on Tony Angelo, Maggie heaved a deep sigh and rolled over on her stomach. She turned her stereo up full blast and stared at the bird's-eye maple headboard of her bed. How would she spend her time if she didn't spend it thinking about Tony Angelo? What else would she have?

Maggie walked over to the edge of her desk, sat down, pulled out a tablet of paper, and wrote at the top of the paper: *Other Interests*. She underlined this with a firm double-stroke of her pencil and wrote a bold *No. 1*. Then she stared at the paper. What was she interested in besides Tony? After some thought, she wrote down: *Watching Old Movies on Television*. But that wasn't a real interest — it was just a way of passing time while she dreamed of Tony. Then she wrote: *Skateboarding*. Realizing that she was too old for skateboarding now, she drew a line through it as well as the old movies. Next she wrote down: *Bicycling*. But it had been almost three months since she'd ridden anywhere on her bicycle at all. She drew a line through *Bicycling*. She looked wildly around her bedroom and remembered that she had papered and painted and decorated the whole bedroom. She wrote down: *Interior Decorating*. At least that was a grown-up interest. But she'd never really gotten around to finishing the ruffle on the bed. She enjoyed pasting the flowered wallpaper on the ceiling, but she'd never made the effort to clean *all* the paste and paint from her floor. Actually, she had lost interest in decorating last summer when she had fallen in love with Tony.

Maggie stood up and walked up and down her bedroom. Pacing and thinking, she wondered if this was what falling in love was supposed to be. Did it destroy all of the ordinary pleasures of life? Vehemently, Maggie shook her head and said aloud, "Of course not, you ninny. No one has to act like this."

With that firm resolution, she went back to her desk, sat down again, and picked up the pencil. She ripped off the top page and wrote: *Ways to Get Tony to Notice Me*. She underlined this with three large, heavy, black lines. Then she wrote: *1. Be Nice to Him*. But even as she was writing that down, she realized that no matter how nice she was, Tony would always think of her as a kid sister. She drew a line through her first possibility. She wrote: *2. Get Beautiful*. She remembered that Tony had walked in on her kicking her legs to the Police, with mayonnaise on her face and hair. Besides, the beauty treatment really hadn't helped much. There was nothing wrong with her looks, but she would never be a knockout the way Denise Meredith was. She drew a line through *Get Beautiful.*

The third possibility that she could think of was, *Flatter Him.* With the thought of flattering him she stopped, chewed on the end of the pencil, and wondered if Tony would like it. What if she suddenly began telling him how wonderful he was? She shook her head and muttered, "No, it wouldn't work. Tony would think I was nuts."

Number four on her list was, *Make Him Jealous.* Even as she was writing it, she was wondering if it would possibly work. Could someone be jealous of a girl he wasn't even interested in? It didn't seem sensible when you looked at it like that, but Maggie knew that jealousy was one of the most important weapons in the arsenal of love — at least, that's how it seemed in old movies. Maybe she could make Tony jealous if she thought it over seriously. Nibbling on the end of the pencil, she stared absently at the painting that was hanging over her desk.

It was a painting that her mother had done two summers ago on Cape Cod, a seascape with birds flying over a deep green sea. Maggie had always loved the painting because it reminded her of that wonderful summer. She also loved the painting because she had learned to use it as a kind of meditation tool. She could stare at the picture of water and birds and grassy beach long enough to solve most of her problems. But this time, as she stared at the painting, she wasn't trying to get away from her problems at all. She was trying to cook up a plan that might possibly make Tony jealous. What could she do? Could she tell him about Charlie Jones, who was always trying to help her with her math homework? No, Tony wouldn't care. There was nothing that would make him jealous unless — unless — maybe she could convince him that some older man was interested in her. If she could get him to believe that, he might see that she was attractive and sophisticated enough to interest men older than he was.

What older man could she get to be interested in her? At that question, Maggie's shoulders slumped. There simply weren't any older men in her life. If there were, they wouldn't be interested in her.

She pushed back her chair, went to the mirror over her dresser, and picked up her hairbrush. As she brushed her short, brown hair, she looked critically at her face. It wasn't the first time that she had observed herself so carefully. In fact, it seemed that about all she'd done this last summer was stare in her mirror and wish that she looked like someone else. If only her hair had slight red or golden highlights. "Golden blond hair would be nice," Maggie said to herself. As she brushed her thick, brown hair, she saw a perfectly shaped oval face with bright green eyes, a turned-up nose, and a light sprinkling of freckles. Absolutely nothing wrong with her looks at all, as her mother was fond of telling her. She even knew that her tall, slim figure was better than most of the girls' in the school. She was a perfectly decent-looking person. Now, if she could only get Tony to see that.

Maggie brushed her lips with a light coral lip-gloss and put on a little mascara before going downstairs to help her mother with the dinner. Tony and Bob would probably be at Tony's house for supper this evening, but you could never tell for sure.

As she worked in the kitchen with her mother, her thoughts went round and round about Tony. She responded to her mother's attempts at conversation with short, dull answers.

Finally, her mother said, "Maggie, pay attention to what I'm saying. You haven't heard a word for the last five minutes."

"Yes, I did," Maggie answered. "You were telling me about Aunt Helen's broken ankle."

"That's what I mean," her mother said, exasperated. "I told you that fifteen minutes ago. I was talking about the commission rate on my new insurance contract." Maggie's mother was an insurance agent. Then she grinned and said sheepishly, "I guess it's too much to ask that a sixteen-year-old take much interest in insurance. But it's time you started listening to these business matters. How are you going to be a success in the world if you spend all your time daydreaming? What do you think about, anyway?"

Maggie answered her mother with a shrug of the shoulders and a general, "Oh, I don't know. Just . . ."

Her mother put the string beans on the table and reached into the refrigerator to pull out the butter as she said happily, "When I was your age I spent a lot of time thinking of boys and stuff like that." She laughed at the memory and said, "You're lucky to be born in a time when you have more important things to think about."

"Do I?" Maggie asked. "What's more important than boys?"

Her mother obviously wasn't taking the conversation very seriously, and she answered quickly, "Oh, I don't know. Insurance rates. What book you read last summer. I just think it must be wonderful to be your age and have the whole world open before you."

"Mom, *you* have the whole world open before you," Maggie said. "You've got a good job, a nice family. You're good-looking. You've got it made."

Her mother nodded her head in agreement and said, "Indeed I do. I've got wonderful children, a husband I love, a wonderful job, and I'm an absolute raving beauty. Isn't it great that you look so much like me?"

Before Maggie could think of a funny reply, the dinner was on the table and the family was sitting down to eat. Bruce and her father were very interested in her mother's conversation about work. As Maggie listened to her mother talk, she wondered if she would ever be as sharp and as sure of herself as her mother was. It seemed as though she had a long way to go.

Bob and Tony came in just as Maggie went to the kitchen for dessert. Her father pointed out that supper was over. Bob said, "We're sorry; we were helping Mrs. Higgens unload her potted plants. Being Good Samaritans."

The excuse seemed to pacify her father, and the boys got plates and silver for themselves from the kitchen. As the rest of the family ate fruit salad and yogurt, Bob and Tony finished off the roast chicken and potatoes.

Maggie had a chance to watch Tony without being obvious. He was so busy eating that she knew he had no idea how closely he was being observed. She saw the way his dark hair seemed to be almost black in the dim dining room lights. It looked so soft and shiny that she wanted to reach out and touch it. Or at least touch his hand. Perhaps trace her finger along the hollow edge of his cheekbone or down the tip of his straight nose.

"What are you thinking, Maggie?" her mother asked sharply. "We've been waiting for your answer for ten minutes."

"What was the question?" Maggie asked in confusion.

As everyone laughed, she realized she'd made herself seem young and foolish again. Tears smarted her eyes, but she held them back. She certainly wasn't going to let anyone see how she hated being laughed at.

She never did find out what the question had been. Supper was over, and her father said to Tony and Bob, "I know it's my night to do the dishes, but I think that you two should help me since you added extra work."

Because Mr. Matthews was such a stickler about organization and routine, Bob and Tony were quick to agree.

Maggie went into the living room with her mother, and they began watching a television program. Soon her father and the boys were finished in the kitchen. Mr. Matthews came in and said, "Bob and I are going to go to the grocery store now. We'll be back in about an hour. Anyone want to put in an extra order before we go?"

Maggie asked for a different kind of cereal she wanted to try. Tony, his eyes twinkling in amusement, suggested, "How about some extra mayonnaise, Mag?"

Maggie picked up the newspaper, folded it into a small paddle, and hit Tony over the head with it. She said, "Bad Tony. Bad Tony," in exactly the tone of voice that she would use to train a feisty puppy.

Tony laughed and ducked his head. Then he settled down comfortably on the couch to watch the television show with Maggie and her mother. About five minutes later, her mother said, "I'm going to make some phone calls now. You can tell me how this show turns out."

As her mother left the room, Maggie's heart began pounding with excitement. She realized that she had a perfect opportunity to make Tony pay attention to her. It was the first time that she had truly been alone with him since the mayonnaise incident three weeks earlier. Determined to make her opportunity work, she stretched languidly and said in what she hoped was a slightly bored and very sophisticated voice, "Did you have a good time with Denise Saturday night?"

"Pretty good," Tony said comfortably. He lifted his long legs up to put them on the hassock that Mrs. Matthews had abandoned when she left the room.

"I just wondered what it was like dating a woman so much younger than you are," Maggie asked Tony.

Tony answered briefly, "Oh, Denise seems pretty grown-up."

Maggie couldn't tell from Tony's tone of voice exactly how good a time he had had with Denise, nor could she tell if he was interested in Denise. She tried to sound casual as she said, "Well, I was just wondering because I'm going to be dating this older guy, and I was sort of putting myself in Denise's place."

Tony didn't flick an eyelash or look even mildly interested as he said, "Oh yeah? You got a date? Who with?"

Maggie said quickly, "You wouldn't know him, but he's quite a bit older than I am."

Tony's attention seemed to be on the television, and he didn't rise to the bait. After some silence, Maggie volunteered the information. "He's twenty-one."

Tony said, "That's nice," and reached over to flick the television dial. Then he sat up straight and turned to look at Maggie.

He asked, "Twenty-one years old? What twenty-one-year-old guy wants to take you out?"

Maggie flushed at the obvious disdain in his

voice. She replied heatedly, "You'd be surprised how many guys want to take me out."

Tony said, "Never mind that. Who's this twenty-one-year-old?"

"He's no one you know," Maggie answered.

"Where did you meet him?" Tony asked.

Maggie's brain raced as she searched for an answer. Unable to come up with anything better, she decided on the plot from an old movie that she'd seen the week before. She said, "I was walking in the park. Then I went into the bookstore, and he followed me in there. We were discussing painters. We both like Gauguin, and from there we just got acquainted."

"Yeah, but who is he? What does he do?" Tony asked.

Maggie was delighted that he had apparently swallowed her story of the bookstore pickup without any difficulty. "Oh, he's an accountant," Maggie answered.

"Why would a twenty-one-year-old accountant want to take out a sixteen-year-old kid like you?" Tony asked, and then a frown crossed his face, and he made a kind of snorting noise. He held up his hand to hold back her answer and said, "No, don't tell me. I can guess why he'd want to take you out. You can't go out with that guy, Maggie. You're too young."

Maggie was delighted that Tony's reaction to her story was as definite as it was. She fought to keep a smile off her face as she said, "It's none of your business who I go out with, Tony Angelo."

40

"Of course it's my business," Tony said. "You're just like a little sister to me."

"I am not your little sister!" Maggie repeated for perhaps the hundredth time that month. "It's bad enough that I have to be Bob and Bruce's sister. I am definitely not yours."

"You may not be my sister," Tony said, "but I think of you as my sister, and I'm going to watch out for you the way I would for my own sister, if I had one. You are not going out with that twenty-one-year-old lecher."

"Lecher? What makes you think he's a lecher?" Maggie said. "You don't even know him."

"All right. You've told me he's twenty-one and he's an accountant. What's his name?" Tony demanded.

"We live in a town of one hundred thousand people," Maggie answered, "and I am sure you wouldn't know the man."

"What's his name?" Tony asked again.

Maggie searched for suitable names. The movie had been an old Rock Hudson and Doris Day flick. She knew that "Rock" would never do, so she thought of one of her favorite old actors, Humphrey Bogart. Out of the blue, she said, "Humphrey. Humphrey Hudson."

"Humphrey Hudson?" Tony said. "Who ever heard of a name like Humphrey Hudson? Are you sure it's his real name?"

"Of course I'm sure it's his real name," Maggie said.

"Well, I guess Humphrey Hudson is a creepy

enough name to fit with a creepy guy like that who wants to prey on the innocence of a sixteen-year-old."

"He was not preying on my innocence," Maggie said in an exasperated tone of voice. "I happen to be very grown-up and sophisticated for sixteen. If you can't see that, it doesn't mean that the rest of the world can't see it."

Tony seemed to consider that idea for a moment. Then he shrugged it off as though he were brushing a fly from the end of his nose. He asked, "Is he in the phone book? I'm going to call him up."

Maggie was surprised at how grim Tony's voice was. She realized he was actually thinking of calling her date up on the telephone. If he went to that telephone, he would discover that there was no Humphrey Hudson. Or worse yet, there might really *be* a Humphrey Hudson. She felt the floor begin to shift beneath her feet, and she realized that she was standing on quicksand. She would have to think fast to get out of this one.

She said, "Tony, he's a perfectly nice man. You have no right to interfere with my personal life, and I am old enough to go out with him. If you'd only look at me, you'd see that I am a grown-up person."

"Does Bob know about this?" Tony asked.

"Of course not," Maggie said. "Bob is only a year and a half older than I am, and he certainly isn't in any position to make a judgment about how I live my life."

"Do your mother and father know about this?" Tony asked.

"They know I have a date," Maggie lied.

"Do they know that your date is twenty-one years old?" Tony said.

Maggie couldn't quite think of an answer to give him because if she told him that her folks knew she was going out with a twenty-one-year-old, there was a good chance that he wouldn't believe her. Her mother and father were strict, as Tony well knew. If she told him that they didn't know, she might have to explain to him why she hadn't told them. Either way, there was a good chance Tony would speak to her parents. That would be awful. She had a very good chance of being exposed as a liar.

She put her hand on Tony's arm and blinked her eyes as she looked at him with what she hoped was her most seductive gaze and said sweetly, "Tony, please don't tell my folks about Humphrey. I'm afraid they wouldn't understand."

"Of course they wouldn't understand," Tony answered sharply. "That's because you've got no business going out with that lecher. I'm going to tell them."

"You keep saying that awful word."

"I know that any twenty-one-year-old who takes out a kid like you can only be interested in one thing. Therefore, you're not going out with him."

"I am so going out with him," Maggie said. Before the conversation could go around again, her father and Bob came in the kitchen door.

Her father called out, "We could use some help with these groceries."

Tony and Maggie automatically rose from the living room couch and started toward the kitchen to help them. As they walked through the dining room, Maggie whispered, "Don't say anything to them. I'll explain it later."

"I'm going to do my duty, Maggie," Tony said. "If it makes you mad, I'm sorry."

Maggie went white as she realized that Tony had every intention of telling her father about her imaginary date with Humphrey Hudson. There was no way out of it. She had to tell Tony the truth. If she didn't, the whole thing would develop into a monstrous embarrassment, involving the whole family.

She stopped in the doorway and whispered to Tony, "Please don't tell them. It was all a lie."

"A lie?" Tony repeated. "You mean he's not twenty-one?"

"That's right. He's not twenty-one."

"Then how old is he?" Tony asked.

"I don't know," Maggie answered.

"Then if you're going out with some guy who you picked up in a bookstore, who you thought might be twenty-one but you're not sure, he could be even older," Tony said in a loud voice. "I'm going to tell your dad right now."

Maggie shook her head again and said, "You don't understand, Tony. It's all a lie."

"What do you mean, 'It's all a lie'?" Tony asked.

"I mean the whole thing is all a lie," Maggie answered. "I made it all up. There is no Humphrey Hudson."

Tony stepped back, looked at Maggie very carefully, and asked in a bewildered voice, "You made the whole thing up, Maggie?"

Maggie nodded her head. Her voice was too tight with embarrassment for her to say anything to him.

Tony stuck his hands in his pockets, seemed to study Maggie very carefully for a moment, then shook his head and said, "No good, Mag. I know you wouldn't make up a long, silly story like that for no reason. You must have been telling the truth, and now you're trying to keep me from spilling the beans. It won't work, Maggie."

"Honest, Tony, I made the whole thing up."

Tony seemed to consider this for a moment and to weigh all the possibilities. Finally he shrugged his shoulders and said, "Maybe you did, but I don't know why. On the other hand, maybe you didn't, but you better not be going out with Humphrey Hudson on Saturday night."

"Honest. I'm not going out with Humphrey Hudson or anyone else on Saturday night," Maggie said. "I'm going to stay right here at home and watch the late, late movie. Just don't tell Mom and Dad that I made up that whole silly story."

Tony whistled lightly through his teeth, leaned back against the wall in the hallway, and said, "Boy, you're really a kid, aren't you, Maggie?"

And then his eyes narrowed lightly and he said, "At least, I think you're just a kid. I'll tell you what; just to make sure that it was all just a childish prank, I'm going to be here Saturday night watching the late, late movie with you. All right?"

Maggie gulped and swallowed and said, "Okay."

"You better be telling me the truth," Tony said. "There better not be any Humphrey Hudson."

Maggie nodded and said, "I am, Tony. I promise you I am," and with that, they walked into the kitchen to help Bob and her dad put away the groceries.

Maggie didn't know whether to laugh or cry. The tall tale she told Tony had made him notice her. At least he seemed to think it was *possible* that someone would be interested in her, if only for the wrong reasons. But her plan had backfired in another way, because now that he thought that she had made up a big lie, he believed that she was younger than ever. But they'd be together Saturday evening. All in all, Maggie decided she had run herself around the Monopoly board and ended up at "Go."

Four

Tony arrived at the Matthewses' house at noon on Saturday. When he got there, Maggie was sitting in her favorite chair in the living room, watching a Jane Russell movie. She had a new *Sweet Sixteen* magazine beside her, and she was reading it during the commercials.

Tony leaned casually against the door frame and said, "Hi, Mag. What's up?"

Maggie turned her head, smiled in what she hoped was a seductive manner, and said, "Not much. Jane Russell is really kind of a dud. I don't know what all the excitement was about."

Tony laughed and said, "You know what you should be when you grow up, Maggie? You should be a film critic, only you'd have to get into a time warp and go backward. You should be a film critic for movies in the nineteen forties and fifties. How would you like that? Huh, kid?"

Maggie drew herself up to her full height, tilted her chin in the air, and said in her most dignified voice, "Number one, Tony Angelo, I'm not a kid, and number two, it happens that watching old movies is very good for the mind. I made an A in English last year."

She expected that Tony would go away, as he usually did, but he didn't seem to be in any hurry. As she watched Jane Russell gallop across the television screen, she became extremely aware of Tony's eyes on her. His gaze seemed to be like an intense beam of light, and she hoped with all her heart that he was finally beginning to actually see her. She held her chin high and tried to look as composed as she possibly could while still maintaining a relaxed posture. It was important for Tony to think that she was wrapped up in the movie.

One thing that Maggie wanted to avoid at all cost was the silly stereotype of being the little girl in love with her older brother's best friend. No one in her family would take her feelings seriously, she was sure, so she tried desperately to cover them up at the same time as she struggled to get Tony to notice her. It was tricky and complicated. That was what had been so humiliating about being caught in the lie last Tuesday. She wished with all her heart that she had never told Tony about Humphrey Hudson.

At the next commercial, Tony asked, "What are your plans for tonight, kid?"

"Don't call me 'kid,' " Maggie replied.

"Okay, Margaret Ann. What are your plans for this evening? It's a simple question. I want a simple answer."

Maggie turned her head slowly and stared at Tony. Did he still think that she might have a date? She said slowly, cautiously, "I told you I made the whole story up, Tony. I'm going to be home tonight."

"Yes, you are," Tony answered softly.

Maggie was startled by the grim determination in his voice, and she saw that his mouth was drawn in a thin, firm line. For the first time, she noticed how square Tony's jaw was. She had always thought of him as being slightly round-faced because of his wide cheekbones and large, brown eyes, but this afternoon his jaw seemed to be as firm and as clenched as Gregory Peck's jaw. She looked carefully at Tony. Did he look a little bit like Gregory Peck?

Quickly she shook her head and thought to herself, no, Tony didn't look like Gregory Peck or Rock Hudson or Humphrey Bogart or any of the other old movie stars that she watched on television. Tony Angelo looked like himself, and that was good enough for her. Her love for Tony was not based on storybook romances or old movies. Her love for Tony was real and had grown out of years of knowing him.

She became more and more aware of his dark brown eyes looking at her. She shifted uncomfortably under his gaze and said in a voice that was surprisingly soft, "I told you it was all a lie,

Tony. I'm not going anywhere tonight. Why don't you believe me?"

Tony seemed to consider that question, and finally he said in a soft, quiet voice, "I'd like to believe you, Maggie, but I can't imagine why you'd tell me such a whopper as that. If you could explain to me why you did it, maybe I could believe you."

He waited expectantly, but there was no possible answer Maggie could give him. She certainly couldn't tell him she had made up the story to make him jealous. She tried to make her voice sound huffy, as she said, "If you don't believe me, you'll just have to sit around and wait. You'll see; I'll be here all evening."

Tony nodded his head as though satisfied and said quickly, "Good. I'll be here, too. What's on the idiot box?"

"Deanna Durbin and Roddy McDowall," Maggie answered promptly.

"No way," Tony said. "How about a game of Monopoly? We could get Bob and Bruce to play."

"Sounds great," Maggie agreed. She was happy that her Humphrey Hudson story would win her an evening with Tony and her brothers. It had been a long time since the four of them sat down to play Monopoly together, but when they had all been younger it had been a common thing for them to do.

Tony seemed satisfied with her answer, and he went out to the garage to work on the car.

Maggie noticed, however, that he came back

into the house to get a drink of water, or for some other reason, just about every half hour.

Finally, at about three o'clock in the afternoon, Maggie decided she had had enough of being watched in this manner. She went to her room, pulled on a sweatshirt and a pair of Levis, and started out through the kitchen to the garage to get her bicycle. In the garage, Tony looked up from under the hood of the car he was working on and said in a sharp, suspicious voice, "Where are you going, Maggie?"

Maggie's voice was exasperated, as she answered, "I'm going for a bicycle ride. It's something lots of people do."

"Alone?" Tony asked.

Maggie said, "You can come with me, but you said you were going to a stock-car race. Why aren't you there?"

Bob pulled himself out from underneath the car, brushed some of the grease onto his coveralls, and said, "That's what I'd like to know. Tony, why aren't we at the races, the way we'd planned?"

Tony jammed his hands into his jeans pockets and looked from his best friend to his best friend's sister. He seemed to be considering his answer very carefully. For one horrible minute Maggie was afraid that Tony was going to tell Bob about her lie, but Tony apparently felt that he should keep her confidence, because he said, "I just wasn't in the mood. We can go next Saturday if you want."

Bob shook his head and said, "I don't know,

Tony. It's just not like you. You don't even *have* moods, and not to go to a stock-car race is definitely not like you. You must be expecting a call from Denise or something. Is she coming over here this afternoon?"

Tony laughed, and Maggie hopped onto her bicycle. Tony said in a soft voice, "This isn't a very good day to go bike riding, Maggie. I wouldn't go if I were you."

Maggie had had enough of Tony's patronizing concern. She whipped her head around and said, "I'm going for a bike ride, Tony."

Tony seemed to consider this, and after a moment he nodded his head and said softly, "I can't stop you, but I can go with you. Come on, Bob, get out your bike and we'll go bike riding with Maggie."

Bob stared at Tony with absolute dismay. "But you just said that we couldn't go to the stock-car races because we had to finish this car today. Now you want to drop everything and go bike riding with Maggie? What's the matter with you?"

"I'll use Bruce's bike," Tony said, ignoring Bob's question, and he went over to the corner of the garage and took Bruce's bicycle out of the bike stand. Bending to inspect the tires, he said, "Looks like Bruce needs some air in his tires. Maggie, we'll have to go down to the gas station first. Okay?"

"Okay," Maggie said. Her stupid story about Humphrey Hudson was somehow turning into a plus for her.

Bob was beginning to look more angry than perplexed, and he said to Tony, "I'm not going."

"Oh, come on," Tony said. "It's a beautiful day. It's time we got out of this dark, dirty garage."

"Sure. Come on," Maggie said, hoping with all her heart that her brother would stick to his first decision.

"Go without me," Bob said to Tony. "I don't know what's got into you, but I don't have to follow every crazy idea that you have. I'll finish cleaning these parts."

Maggie was feeling joyful and full of life as she pointed her bicycle out of the garage and wheeled down the driveway. She didn't even turn to look and see if Tony was behind her, but aimed straight for the corner gas station.

When they got to the station, Jim Thompson was sitting in his black Camero with the bright red upholstery. He seemed to be flirting with the girl who worked as gas station attendant, and Maggie and Tony rode right by him. As Tony bent over to put air in the tires, Jim called, "Hey, Maggie, come on over here."

Maggie was surprised that Jim would call to her. He sat behind her in English class and sometimes he said hello, but they weren't really friends. Jim was a senior, repeating tenth-grade English for the third time, and he had a reputation of being more interested in women than in grammar. Since Maggie had been at Hudson High, he'd gone steady with three different girls, and everyone said he always had two or three other girl-friends on the side.

Maggie had never liked Jim much because he always seemed so slick and self-centered, but she went over to talk to him anyway. He was leaning out of his car window and smiling at her. He had a lot of teeth, and Maggie had the feeling she was supposed to be dazzled by his charm as he said, "Hi, sweetheart, what are you up to?"

"Bike riding," Maggie said. She wished she could think of something sharper to say.

Jim was still smiling, and he motioned with his hand, saying, "Come a little closer, sweetheart."

Maggie felt like a fool, but she stepped up closer to the car. She leaned on her bicycle as though she were about to make a fast getaway.

Jim reached out and touched her bare arm with his fingertips. Running his hand up her arm lightly, he asked, "Why don't you park the bicycle and come for a ride with me?"

Maggie pulled back and said, "I've got to go." Then she turned and walked her bicycle over to Tony's. Tony was frowning when she came up, and he asked sharply, "What did that creep want?"

"Nothing," Maggie said. She suddenly felt very defensive — as though she'd done something wrong.

"What did he say to you?" Tony demanded.

"He asked me to go for a ride with him," Maggie said. She was amazed to see how angry Tony's face was. "It was nothing," she said quickly. "Forget it. Jim's in my English class. We're friends."

Tony frowned and made a face to indicate his disapproval. "He's a creep," Tony said again. When Maggie didn't answer, he seemed to be satisfied.

Tony jumped on his bike and said, "Come on, Maggie, if you're coming." His voice was full of irritation.

She flashed Tony a brilliant smile and said in a sweet voice, "Jim is really a lovely person when you get to know him."

Ignoring her, Tony pointed his bicycle to the right and asked, "Want to go to the lake?"

"That would be great," Maggie said.

She pedaled off in the direction of the lake. It was one of those golden September days in Indian summer. The sky was a bright, clear blue, and there were a few small, white clouds frolicking as though they were baby kittens playing. Though the air was cooler than it would have been in the summertime, the sun made the day very warm, and the light, cool, fall breeze felt good on Maggie's skin as she pedaled for the lake. September was one of her favorite times of the year because it was what she thought of as an in-between time. Though some of the maples were turning red and yellow, most of the trees were still a bright green. Maggie knew that they would be turning in the next week or two, because the nights were sharp and crisp. *But today is summer*, Maggie told herself as she pedaled fiercely in the sunshine. In a way, this ride to the lake with Tony would make up for some of what she had come to think of as her lost summer. A wave of sadness washed over Maggie, and she wished that she had not wasted her time watching old movies. Though she hated to admit that her brothers and Tony had been right, she realized that the summer had passed for her as though she were in a dream or daze.

They pedaled the four miles to the lake without talking. Part of the time Maggie was in the lead and part of the time Tony was. Maggie couldn't decide whether she liked having the feeling of Tony following her more than she liked following him, watching his brown hair shine in the sunshine. His striped T-shirt seemed to glow in the late afternoon light as romantically as a Mexican caballero's bright, striped blanket.

When they got to the lake, it was almost deserted. They parked their bicycles in the rack and there were only three others there. Tony laughed and said, "When school starts, summer closes."

"You're right," Maggie said. She ran lightly down the sloping hill to the edge of the lake and stood with her hands on her hips, her legs spread apart, looking across the lake to the small island that sat in its center. As Tony walked softly down to join her, Maggie turned to him and smiled, asking, "Do you remember the summer that Bob and Bruce left you on the island?"

Tony nodded. "I was scared. I thought they'd never come back for me."

"I was scared, too," Maggie said.

Tony's dark brown eyes lightened, and the skin around his eyes crinkled as he looked at her warmly. He reached up, put his arm around her shoulder, and hugged her to him for a moment.

He said, "I remember, Maggie. You cried. If you hadn't cried, they probably never would have turned around and come after me. I'd still be sitting out there in the middle of that island, wouldn't I?"

Maggie leaned her head lightly against Tony's shoulder. Tony's hand on her arm, his arm resting around her shoulder, her head on his shoulder, seemed to her to be the most enchanting thing that could happen.

She lifted her face to his and said in a soft whisper, "I would have rescued you, Tony."

He laughed and squeezed her shoulder, then bent down and brushed her cheek with a light kiss. "I know you would have, kid."

With that, he turned and started back toward his bicycle, calling to her, "Come on, Maggie. We'll be late for supper."

But Maggie was in no hurry to move. She was standing, looking at the lake, enjoying the warmth of Tony's kiss. Would Tony have kissed her like that if he wasn't interested in her at all? Though she was sure that Tony's kiss was intended to be a brotherly one, wasn't it evidence of a deeper interest? She could still feel the warm pressure of his hand against her shoulder, the light brush of his lips against her cheek. She whispered to the wind, "Oh, Tony, I love you so. Why can't you see me?"

Tony called from the top of the sloping hill, "Hurry up, Mag. Let's go."

Maggie turned and ran lightly up the hill, hopped on her bicycle, and pedaled furiously toward home. As she rode, she dreamed of a glorious future with Tony. At least, Maggie wanted desperately to believe in that possibility.

When they got back to the house, Tony got off his bicycle, turned, and said to Maggie with a note of surprise in his voice, "That was fun. We haven't done that in a long time."

"No, we haven't," Maggie answered, and she tried to keep her voice as comradely as possible. "We could do it again next Saturday," she offered tentatively.

Tony shook his head and grinned, "Better not. If I cancel two Saturdays in a row, Bob will never forgive me. As it is, he just thinks I'm slightly wacky."

"Thanks for not telling him about Humphrey Hudson," Maggie said.

"No sense telling anyone until something happens," Tony answered shortly.

Maggie didn't know what else to say and so she went into the house to help her brother Bruce prepare supper. As she and Bruce worked in the kitchen they talked about Bruce's first week at college. He was going to the state university and would be able to come home every weekend.

Maggie said to him, "You know, I didn't think I would, but I missed you a lot this week."

Bruce was chopping onions and carrots to put in the salad as Maggie turned the hamburgers in the skillet. He nodded his head in quick agreement and said, "I was so busy I didn't miss anyone until Thursday, and by that time I knew that I only had one more day. But you know, Mag, I am glad that I didn't go farther away after all."

"Are you?" Maggie asked. "I still think I'd like to go to a western college."

"Don't decide yet," Bruce advised. "You have two more years before you have to make up your mind. Just have a good time in high school."

"I wish I were a junior," Maggie said. "It isn't fair that I'm two years behind Bob and Tony. Bob's not two years older than I am. I'm thinking about going to summer school for the next two years and skipping a year."

"Why are you in such a rush?" Bruce asked.

"Oh, I don't know," Maggie answered. "It just seems so important to get on with life. Do you understand what I mean?"

Bruce shook his head and laughed as he said, "High school is life. Whatever you may think, what you're doing in high school is just as important as anything you'll be doing in college."

"But isn't it a lot different?" Maggie asked. "I should think college would be so exciting, and everyone would treat you as though you're a grown-up. I get so tired of being treated as though

I'm a kid. I just think it would be wonderful to be a college girl."

"Don't wish your life away," Bruce said. "Here, will you help me take the potatoes out of the oven?"

"But doesn't everyone seem adult and sophisticated?" Maggie asked, as she pulled the baked potatoes onto the oval platter and put the hamburger patties beside them.

"You'd be surprised," Bruce answered. "Some of my roommates don't look any older than you do. And a lot of them don't act as grown-up as you, either," he added.

"But you did make some friends?" Maggie asked anxiously.

Bruce put his arm around her shoulder and squeezed her exactly as Tony had done earlier that day. He bent and kissed her on the forehead as he said, "Don't worry, Maggie. I'm making friends. I'm having a good time. College is wonderful. I'm just telling you not to be in such a hurry to get through your life. Enjoy every day. Live a day at a time."

Maggie laughed and poked her older brother in the ribs as she said, "That's very impressive, Bruce. One week as a philosophy major and the only thing you can come up with is a cornball cliché like, 'Live one day at a time.' "

Bruce didn't have a chance to answer, because the Matthews family and Tony were too eager to hear all about his first week's experiences at school. During dinner, Bruce told them all about his new classes and what he thought of his professors. He described some of the people that he had met in school and talked a little bit about his roommates.

Maggie was particularly fascinated by the idea of living in a coed dorm. She thought it must be wonderful to meet so many different kinds of people. Bruce said that his roommates came from six different states, as far away as California and Texas. "I'm the only one from Massachusetts," he said. "In fact, the only other easterner is Alan. He's from New York City."

"I've never met anyone who grew up in New York City," Maggie said wistfully. "Does he live in Manhattan?"

Bruce nodded. "On Fifth Avenue and Seventy-sixth Street. He grew up there with his grandmother and uncle. I guess they're very wealthy. His uncle is an investor or something. He's a fine arts major and wants to make movies. In fact, he's crazier about movies than you are."

When Maggie asked if Alan was terribly sophisticated, Bruce laughed and said, "Well, at least he thinks he is, but you'll get a chance to see for yourself one of these days. I'll probably invite him home sometime."

After supper, Tony and Bob helped Bruce and Maggie clear the table and do the dishes. They were very anxious to finish up so that they could get into the Monopoly game.

As they were putting the last dishes away, Maggie said, "If Bruce is going to be the banker, how about I make some popcorn?"

"Don't put any butter on it," Bob warned. "You'll get the board all greasy."

Maggie laughed and said, "Nothing could happen to that Monopoly game that hasn't already happened."

"I'll melt the butter," Tony said. "Bruce, you set up the money and we'll be with you in a jiffy. Right, little sis — no, no. Right, Maggie?"

Gratified that Tony had corrected himself mid-word and apparently was trying very hard not to call her "little sister" anymore, Maggie agreed quickly and pulled the popcorn down off the shelf. She worked as quickly as she could and had a big bowl popped by the time Bruce and Bob had cleared the table and laid out the Monopoly board.

As they sat down to play, Bruce volunteered, "You know, this game is really passé. Everyone at college is playing bridge or Dungeons and Dragons."

"Around here we play chess and Monopoly," Maggie said. "I guess that makes us hopelessly old-fashioned."

"Something like that," Bruce agreed happily as he jammed a handful of popcorn into his mouth.

All four of them threw themselves into the game, yelling, arguing, laughing. Maggie wondered if their enjoyment was because it had been a long time since they had all sat down together. This last year, since she'd fallen in love with Tony, she'd gradually withdrawn from her brothers. In her zeal to get rid of the little-sister image, she realized that she had perhaps lost out on some fun. *But it hasn't been just my fault*, Maggie thought. Bruce had been busy all year getting ready for his college board exams and studying, doing the extra reading for his philosophy courses this fall. Bob and Tony seemed to spend most of their time out in the garage. *We're all getting older.*

The idea that they were getting older and that things were changing suddenly made Maggie feel sad. Her face must have shown it because Bob looked up from his end of the board and asked, "What's wrong, Maggie?"

"I was just thinking about something," Maggie answered quickly and put a smile on her face.

Even the momentary change of expression seemed to have been enough to remind Tony why they were playing Monopoly this evening. Tony looked at his watch and then glanced sharply at Maggie as he asked, "Expecting a call?"

"I told you I wasn't!" Maggie said. Her voice displayed her frustration and embarrassment.

Tony looked at her face carefully for a moment, as though he were trying to read her mind.

As she felt Tony's warm, brown eyes on her, she could feel his kiss on her cheek again. A slight tremor ran through her body. She shivered, and Tony asked, "You cold?"

"A little," Maggie answered. "I think I'll get a sweater." With that she stood up and went toward her bedroom to get her sweater.

As she came out of her bedroom, carrying a white sweater, she was dismayed to find Tony standing beside her bedroom door. She bumped into him as she came out and looked up at him and said, "What are you doing here?"

"I just wanted to make sure you weren't going to make a phone call," Tony explained patiently.

For some reason that she didn't quite understand, Maggie's reaction to Tony's distrust was deep sadness. She felt tears well up into her eyes, and she said, "Tony, I told you; I'm not expecting a phone call!"

As though on cue, the telephone rang. Tony's face changed, and he fixed his sharp, dark eyes on Maggie as he said, "No one's going to call you tonight?"

"It won't be for me," Maggie answered as she went back to the kitchen. As she was halfway through the living room, her mother called out, "Maggie, it's for you."

Maggie went into the dining room where the telephone was and said in a small voice, "Hello."

"Hi, Maggie. What are you doing tonight?" a voice from the other end asked. It was a deep male voice that was satin-smooth.

For a moment, Maggie could only think of Charlton Heston's voice. She blinked her eyes and asked, "Who is this?"

"This is Jim Thompson."

"Hi." Maggie tried to keep her voice from showing surprise.

For a minute she wondered if he might not be calling about the homework assignment in English.

But Jim obviously wasn't calling her about homework at eight o'clock on Saturday night, Maggie corrected herself quickly.

"I was driving around your neighborhood and I thought maybe I'd give you a ring — see if you're busy this evening."

"Busy?" Maggie repeated stupidly. She was extremely aware of the fact that Tony was standing just at her elbow.

"I thought maybe you'd like to go for a ride with me. We could go out to the lake — something like that." His deep, vibrant voice held just a hint of the romantic as he continued, "Beautiful girl like beautiful moonlit night? Come on, Maggie. You're not doing anything else."

Tony whispered, "Get rid of him."

"Oh, but I am," Maggie said quickly. "I have a date. He's standing here right beside me," Maggie said.

"Oh," Jim answered abruptly. "Who with?"

"Tony. Tony Angelo," Maggie said, and then she added, "But I'd love to go out with you some other time."

As she said this, Tony's hand reached up to take the phone away from her.

Maggie stepped back, pushed Tony away, and frowned fiercely at him as she said in a light, flirtatious voice, "Call me some other time, will you, Jim?"

"Sure, honey," Jim answered, and Maggie heard the phone click in her ear.

She turned to Tony and said, "That was Jim Thompson. He wanted me to go for a ride."

Tony's face was one of pure disgust as he answered, "And you told him to call you some other time. Of all the stupid things you could have done, Maggie, that is the most. Now you'll have that creep chasing you until Christmas."

"Maybe I'll let him catch me," Maggie said lightly.

Tony did not laugh. In fact, he said, "Let's get back to the game." As they walked back to the kitchen, he muttered, "Humphrey Hudson wasn't bad enough. Now it's Jim Thompson."

As they went back into the kitchen and took their places at the Monopoly table, Bob looked up and said, "Who was that?"

"Jim Thompson," Maggie answered. "He wanted me to go out."

Bob snorted and said, "Well, you're not going out with him, that's for sure."

"I'll go out with whomever I please," Maggie snapped back.

Bruce reached over, took a handful of popcorn, and said, "Thompson. Isn't he that tall, dark guy with all the teeth?"

"That's the one," Bob answered. "He's got too much experience for Maggie. She's not going out with him."

"Certainly not," Tony chimed in.

Bruce looked at Maggie and asked quietly, "But you told him no, didn't you, Maggie?"

"I told him no," Maggie said, "but not because I wanted your permission. I'll go out with anyone I want to anytime I want to. You're not my parents, and you have no reason to boss me around."

"They're just trying to look out for you," Bruce said softly.

"I don't care," Maggie replied. "I'm sick and tired of everyone telling me what to do all the time. I'm the youngest but that doesn't mean that everyone gets to treat me like a baby all the time."

"Nobody's treating you like a baby," Tony said. He sounded very irritated. "We're just telling you that Thompson is no one a nice girl would want to go out with. You're a nice girl so you're not going out with him."

"You think that you have a right to boss me around the way you did when I was five years old," she said to Tony, "but you don't! Nobody does. I'll go out with Jim if I want to."

"Oh, let it go," Bob said. "He'll never call her back. You know Thompson; if they don't say yes the first time, he goes off and looks for someone else. Besides that, he wouldn't really be interested in Maggie."

That was what it took to make Maggie absolutely furious. She slammed the Monopoly dice down on the table and said, "That settles it. I'm inviting Jim to Marian's party next Saturday night."

Tony opened his mouth to say something else, but Bob shook his head at his best friend in warning and said, "Lay off her, Tony. She's mad now. You don't want to make her so mad she'd really do a dumb thing like that."

Tony looked as though he wanted to argue, but he didn't. Instead, he said, "I'll give you a thousand dollars for Boardwalk, Maggie."

Maggie crossed her arms over her chest, leaned back in her chair, and glared at Tony. "You couldn't begin to pay enough to get Boardwalk from me tonight."

Tony laughed and tried to make light of her obvious anger, but Maggie was not that easily appeased. Though she spent the rest of the evening playing Monopoly with the boys, she was very careful not to get into any kind of serious conversation with them. She certainly did not want to discuss Humphrey Hudson or Jim with them. Tony probably believed Humphrey Hudson was an imaginary character, but he was obviously dismayed at Jim's interest. But she didn't care anymore. She was so mad at Tony and Bruce and Bob that she was ready to do anything, no matter how drastic.

The first thing on Monday morning, in third period English class, she would invite Jim to go to the party. She wasn't going to tell them that right now, though. If she did, they would protest to her parents and it would be forbidden. Better just to ask Jim. Her anger was mixed with amusement as she imagined the horrified expressions on the faces of Tony and Bob and Bruce when they saw her walk out the door next Saturday night with Jim.

As she imagined the impression she was going

to make, she began to worry a little bit. Maybe Jim already had a date for next Saturday night. All she could do was to wait until Monday morning and hope for the best.

Five

On Monday morning, Jim looked surprised when Maggie invited him to the party. He asked, "Who's going to be there?"

"Oh, just some kids from school," Maggie answered. "You'll know some, but not all of them. You don't have to go if you don't want to."

Jim flashed his wonderful white teeth at Maggie and ran his fingers through his black hair as he said, "Sure, honey. It will be fun to check out the local high school scene again."

Maggie decided right then that she really didn't like Jim at all and she was sorry that she had invited him to the party. Somehow, it didn't seem fair to use one man to attract another, even if the man she was using for bait was as conceited as Jim.

She waited until Wednesday to mention casually to her parents at the dinner table that she had a date for the party next Saturday night.

Her brother Bob was just bringing in the dessert when Maggie said, "I've invited a boy named Jim Thompson to go with me to Marian's party on Saturday night."

Bob put the plate of hot gingerbread on the table with a thud and said, "You're not serious about going out with that creep, are you?"

Maggie ignored Bob and went on with her conversation with her parents. She said, "Marian's having about ten girls from the sophomore class and we're all going to watch *King Kong* on television at midnight, so I won't be home until about two. All right?"

Her mother and father looked at each other and then nodded their heads simultaneously. As they were nodding their heads yes, Bob was saying in a loud voice, "No. Don't let her do it, Mom. Thompson is a terrible guy. Don't let her go out with him."

Maggie's mother said quietly to Bob, "I'm sure that Maggie has good judgment in her friends, and she's certainly old enough to pick her own date."

At the same time that Maggie's mother was expressing her confidence in Maggie, her father asked softly, "What about it, Mag? Is Bob right? Is this fellow someone you should be going out with?"

"Oh, Daddy," Maggie answered. "You know how high school kids are. Jim does have a reputation for being more sophisticated than some of Bob's friends, but I'm sure he'll treat me okay."

Her father looked mildly doubtful, despite her assurances, but he didn't say anything else. It surprised Maggie that her parents didn't put up more of a protest after Bob made such a case against Jim. It also made her feel a little guilty because, she had to admit, she really didn't know much about Jim except that he thought he was a real lady-killer. A lot of girls thought he was cute but she didn't. At the same time, though, her parents' attitude pleased her, and she thought they must be beginning to accept her as an adult who was able to make her own decisions. She was glad about their confidence in her — despite the fact that in the case of Jim, it was mildly misplaced. Not that she expected to have any trouble with him. She was pretty sure that Bob was exaggerating when he said Jim was so awful.

Maggie was sure Bob would have told Tony about her date but when she saw Tony on Thursday night, he only said, "Hi, kid." Then he walked through the room as though it were no different from any other evening.

On Friday, Tony had supper with the Matthews family, and Maggie waited patiently for him to say something about Jim. When he seemed absolutely oblivious to Maggie, she realized that he didn't intend to say or do anything. She was disappointed and decided his lack of protest meant that he really wasn't interested in her at all.

After supper, Tony and Bob went out on a double date — Bob was dating Judy for the second Friday night this month, and Maggie had a terrible feeling that Tony was taking Denise out again. But she didn't ask. As the two boys walked out the front door, Mrs. Matthews looked up from her book and said, "Have a nice time."

Maggie's mouth was too dry and cottony with disappointment for her to chime in. She continued to watch the old movie on television and pretended that she didn't know they were leaving.

The next evening it was Maggie's turn. Bob and Tony were spending the evening at home together. They were reading a service manual for the old Volkswagen that they had just bought to rebuild. Maggie at least had the pleasure of knowing that Tony would see her leave the house on the arm of Jim Thompson.

Perhaps because she knew Tony was going to be there when Jim picked her up, Maggie was extremely nervous while she dressed for this date. She would ordinarily have chosen to wear pants and a sweater to a party at her friend's house, but this party was more a dramatic part in her campaign to capture Tony than it was a real party. Slacks didn't seem to be appropriate. She found the dark green dress that she had bought for last year's Christmas party. It was a beautiful dress, and Maggie had only worn it that one time. This evening as she zipped the dress up and stepped in front of her mirror to inspect her reflection, she realized that she had grown at least an inch since last year. She must be at least five feet eight inches tall now, and the sleeves seemed shorter, too. Maggie pushed the long sleeves partway up her wrists and twirled lightly, looking at herself in the mirror. She loved the way the soft, green velvet fit her slim torso and then flared out gently over her hips and legs. It was a wonderful dress for dancing, and she felt a little like Ginger Rogers getting ready to go out with Fred Astaire.

Maggie wondered if Jim was a good dancer, then she decided that of course he would be. It might be fun to go out on a date with someone who was as smooth and sophisticated as Jim was. At least, she was going to try very hard to make the evening fun, she promised herself.

She picked up some thin, brass bracelets that she'd bought in a boutique in New York City when she was twelve years old. There were seven very thin Indian bracelets, which she pulled over her left hand, and then she put on some large, brass, Indian earrings with dark red glass beads. Again, very critically, she looked at her reflection in the mirror and decided that with her soft, black shoes, she looked quite as grown-up and sophisticated as any college girl.

There wasn't much she could do about her short, dark hair. She wished for a moment that it were longer so that she could pull it up in a bun or wear it in one of those flowing cascades that were so popular in shampoo commercials. But even though her hair was an ordinary brown in an ordinary cut, she thought that her final appearance was really quite spectacular.

Pleased with herself, Maggie left her bedroom and walked into the living room where Tony and

Bob were reading the service manual. She was dressed thirty minutes before Jim was supposed to pick her up, but that didn't bother her at all. In fact, it was part of the plan.

As she walked into the living room, her mother said, "You look lovely, dear. Would you like to wear my pearls?"

Maggie shook her head quickly and raised her hand to the high collar. Pearls would spoil the whole effect.

As she raised her hand, the brass bracelets tinkled like little bells, and Maggie was glad she'd decided to wear them this evening. Tony looked up from the service manual for a moment and said, "Hi Mag." Then he went back to studying his parts book.

Bob also seemed much more engrossed in the automobile instructions than in his sister's appearance. Maggie was disappointed that neither boy gave her any more attention. Their initial resistance to her dating Jim seemed to have disappeared totally and she didn't quite understand why.

When Jim rang the bell, Mrs. Matthews opened the door and insisted that he come in. Maggie was mortified as her mother said, "Now, Jim. I understand that you and Maggie will be at the party until quite late. Maggie tells me the movie begins at midnight and will be over at one-thirty in the morning. It takes about ten minutes to get from Marian's house to our house by automobile. I expect that you will have Maggie at home by one-forty-five in the morning. Right?"

Maggie's toes began to blush and the color flashed through her body, finally settling on her cheeks, which were purple with embarrassment by the time her mother had finished this speech. She might have known. No wonder Tony and Bob seemed so disinterested. They had turned it all over to her mother to handle. No one could sound as firm or authoritative as Mary Matthews when she chose to do so.

Instead of looking amused, Jim looked mildly frightened. He stammered out the most courteous thing that Maggie had ever heard him say. "Don't worry, Mrs. Matthews. I'll bring her home on time."

"One-forty-five. Is that clear, Jim?" Mrs. Matthews spoke in her firmest voice.

Jim nodded quickly and asked Maggie, "Are you ready?"

Maggie was almost frozen with embarrassment, and she would have liked to have turned and run back into her bedroom. What good did it do to put on your most grown-up dress to look sophisticated if your mother was going to spoil it all before you got out the front door? She glanced over to where Bob and Tony sat huddled in the corner with their service manuals, and she could see that both boys were fighting hard to keep from laughing. It had all been a trick! She needn't have congratulated herself for the fact that her family was treating her in a more grown-up manner. They were still treating her like a child, and worse yet, they had all conspired against her. But Maggie did not turn and run back into her bedroom. She was determined not to let them know how hurt she was. Instead, she picked up the Mexican rebozo that she had chosen to wear over the green dress and said, "Don't worry about a thing, Mother." She kissed her mother on the cheek and walked out the front door with her head held as high as she could manage.

Maggie followed Jim out to his fancy, black car. He didn't say anything, and she couldn't think of any words of her own, so it was very silent as he turned on the ignition and drove away from the house. Finally, Maggie cleared her throat and said, "You have a beautiful car, Jim."

"Yeah," Jim agreed.

There was more silence, and Maggie tried again. She said, "Do you have any hobbies? I mean, do you fix up cars or play sports or anything?" She knew her question was dumb, but she really didn't know anything at all about Jim. The idea of spending a whole evening with him suddenly terrified her.

He laughed and slowed down the car, pulling into a small parking space beside the city park. He turned off the ignition and turned to face her, his white teeth shining brightly as he lit a cigarette, then offered her a puff. She shook her head no.

"Not old enough to smoke?" he teased. "How old are you, Maggie?"

"Almost seventeen," she said.

"I'm nineteen," Jim said. "Almost twenty." Then he frowned as though he'd told her too much. She realized that Jim must have stayed behind in school more than one year. She wondered what that felt like.

He held the cigarette with one hand, blowing smoke out slowly, and let his other arm drop casually along the back of the seat of the car. Maggie realized that he was about to put his arm around her. She leaned forward, looking out the window of the car as she said, "Oh, look. I think that was Bud and Barbara. They're going to be at the party, too. Let's follow them."

"Let's not," Jim said quickly.

Maggie turned to see if he was kidding or angry. She still couldn't tell because his face seemed to have only one expression — a big smile. She wondered if he smiled when no one was around. She said, "The party starts at eight."

"Then it will have to start without us," Jim said and pulled her close to him.

Before she quite understood what was happening, she was being kissed by Jim. His breath tasted of cigarette smoke, and her only reaction was to want to get away as fast as possible. She pulled back quickly and said firmly, "I want to go to the party."

"Don't be such a kid," Jim said. "I thought you were more grown-up than that." He leaned forward to grab her again, but Maggie turned so that she was twisted into the corner of the car. Her voice was a little frightened but very strong as she said, "Jim, I invited you to a party, and it's time to go now."

Jim laughed and asked, "You scared of me? Don't be scared, Maggie. I won't hurt you. I just want us to get acquainted. Come on over here, honey."

"If you don't start the car, I'm getting out," Maggie said breathlessly. She wished with all her heart that she'd never invited Jim out. He was going to be a problem from the very start. She wished she'd simply avoided him.

Jim must have sensed that she was serious, because he started the engine and drove back onto the street. As he drove, he turned to Maggie and said, "Are you ready for a swinging evening, Maggie? I am."

Maggie was not quite sure what "swinging evening" meant to Jim. But since she felt that she had looked so young and awkward a minute ago, she managed a small smile and said, "Sure, Jim."

"Okay, kid. Let's go."

Jim was smiling again. Maggie thought of sharks, and she asked herself, *What am I doing here?*

When Jim turned the wrong way and she saw that they weren't even heading toward Marian's house, Maggie's heart began to thump. She asked, "Jim, where are we going?"

"Oh . . . I thought we'd drive down by the lake and then maybe over to a little place I know in the Berkshires, not too far from here. It's called

Mama's Hideaway Lounge. How does that sound, honey?"

Jim dropped his arm on the backseat again, and before she knew it, Maggie felt his hand on her shoulder. He pulled her slightly toward him.

Resisting with a firm pull in the opposite direction, Maggie tried as best she could to imitate her mother's voice. She said, "Jim, I promised Marian I'd go to the party. We'd better get there or else she'll be worried."

Jim laughed and said, "Oh, don't be such a baby, Maggie. I thought you were a grown-up girl. You don't have to do exactly what your mama tells you all the time, do you? Don't you ever want to be an independent person?"

"And do what you tell me?" Maggie said quickly.

It was funny to hear Jim say out loud some of the things that she had been thinking only a short time before. Coming from Jim Thompson, they sounded ridiculous.

She said, "My mother and father are strict, and I have to go to the party if that's where I said I was going."

Jim frowned and said, "I don't understand why you invited me. You must have known that I wouldn't be interested in going to that kids' party. Come on, Maggie. Don't be like that."

As he talked, he took another turn, and Maggie realized that they were heading toward the out-skirts of town. There was no sense allowing this to go any farther. She said, "Jim, turn the car around and take me to Marian's house right this minute."

Jim just laughed and stepped on the gas. His arm circled her shoulder more tightly, and he tried to pull her closer to him. He said, "I know what you want, baby. You want a strong, masterful man like me to take charge of the situation."

Maggie was no longer frightened, but she *was* angry. His hand on her shoulder felt like sticky glue, and she wanted to throw it off.

She glanced sideways at Jim and wondered why some girls seemed to like him so much. *Maybe they don't*, Maggie thought suddenly. *Maybe the whole thing is just an act. Maybe he's really insecure and frightened.* That could be true, she decided, but she wasn't going to stick around long enough to find out.

Maggie waited until they got to the next stoplight. As the car slowed for the light, she put her hand on the door and said, "Either you turn around and drive me back to Marian's party or I'm getting out of the car right now."

Jim looked surprised and seemed not to know how to react to her threat. He laughed shortly and said, "Oh, don't be so dramatic, Maggie."

She asked, "Are you turning around?"

"Of course not," Jim said. "I told you, we're going to have a good time. We'll drive over the mountain to the Berkshires. We'll go to Mama's Hideaway Lounge. We'll dance. We'll have a few beers."

Maggie pressed on the door handle. The door

opened, and she stepped out of the car. It seemed so simple. She half-expected that Jim would try to persuade her to change her mind. Perhaps he would even offer to drive her back to the party. But Jim sat behind the wheel, looking at Maggie walk away. She didn't turn to look back until she was across the street and on the sidewalk. Then she turned and was surprised to see that Jim was still sitting behind the wheel, staring straight ahead at the mountains.

Maggie started walking and kept on walking without turning around again. She walked for what seemed like a long time and finally came to the corner that she would have to turn to go home or to go to Marian's house. She stopped, leaned against the lamp post, and tried to decide what to do. It was nine o'clock. If she went home, Bob and Tony would probably laugh at her. They were laughing when she left. On the other hand, did she want to go to the party without a date? How would she explain that she had left Jim on Highway 9?

She stood there a long time, trying to make up her mind. Both choices seemed terrible. She never did really make up her mind because Bruce drove past her, slowed down, backed up, leaned out of the car, and called, "Hey, Maggie, what are you doing standing on the street corner?"

Maggie had no choice but to say, "I'm just on my way home."

"Well, come on. Get in," Bruce said.

Maggie saw that he had three people with him.

There was a young woman sitting beside him in the front seat, and a young man and woman in the back seat. Maggie shook her head quickly and said, "No. You were going somewhere, weren't you? The folks don't even know you're in town this weekend."

Bruce laughed and said, "Well, I'm not in town. It's just that we decided to drive into the city for pizza. Come on. We'll take you home."

Before she could argue, Maggie found herself squeezed beside a slim, young college girl who said, "Oh, that dress you have on is so pretty. I'll bet you're going to a party, aren't you?"

"Was," Maggie said, and as she said it, she realized that this was the first of many explanations she would have to make.

Bruce introduced the young man in the car as Alan, his roommate. Maggie looked at him seriously. She saw that he was tall and dark with a rather large nose and prominent Adam's apple. Maggie thought he looked somehow more awkward and seemed younger than she had expected Bruce's roommate to be. A fine arts major who planned to go into film should have had a more sophisticated look than Alan did, and suddenly, Maggie thought of Woody Allen.

She smiled at him and said she was glad to meet him, just as the car drove up to her doorstep. Mustering all the courage she had, Maggie stepped out of the car and walked as regally as she could up the front steps of her house. She opened the front door and walked into the living room. To her overwhelming relief, Tony was not there. Bob sat reading the same service manual.

Maggie asked, "Where are the folks? Where's Tony?"

At the same time, Bob asked, "What are you doing home?" Then he said, "The folks went to the movies. Tony went home. What are you doing home?"

Maggie sighed and flopped down on the couch. She said, "Well, go ahead and laugh. I guess I have it coming."

"What did he do to you?" Bob demanded, his voice as stern and irate as a sheriff in an old western.

It was Maggie who laughed as she replied, "He didn't do anything to me. I guess I did it to him."

"What happened?" Bob demanded again. "Where's Jim?"

"The last time I saw Jim, he was driving down Route 9 toward Mama's Hideaway Lounge in the Berkshires," Maggie said. As she said that she turned to her brother and sighed, "Oh, Bob, you were right. He's an awful guy and I had no business going out with him. So you can laugh at me if you want. I know I've got it coming."

"I'm not laughing at you," Bob said. "As long as you're all right, Maggie. That's all that's important."

"I only did it because I wanted to seem grown-up and impress Tony," Maggie said, and then she quickly made that into, "Tony and you."

Bob nodded his head understandingly and said

in a soft voice, "I guess it's hard being the little sister, isn't it, Maggie?"

"Promise you won't tell anyone about this evening?" Maggie begged. "If Tony asks you, just tell him you guess I had a pretty good time. Don't tell him that I walked out on my date at nine o'clock in the evening. Do you promise? Will you do that for me?"

Bob seemed to be considering the request. Maggie hoped that he would be able to see how important it was to her without her having to explain exactly *why* it was so important. It was with great relief that she saw Bob nod his head gently and say, "Okay, Mag. I promise. Tony won't know a thing about this."

Six

Maggie always thought of the date with Jim Thompson as the date that changed her life. Even though Jim wouldn't speak to her at school on Monday morning, she was not sorry that she walked out on him. In fact, walking out on Jim gave her a sense of being able to control her own destiny in a way that she had never experienced before. She used the week that followed as a week to examine her life and to see what she was doing wrong.

She gave a lot of serious thought to her relationship with Tony Angelo. In fact, she spent more time thinking about Tony than perhaps ever before, but her thinking was tinged with new maturity and seriousness.

By the end of the week, she had definitely decided that no matter how attractive she found Tony, she was through chasing him. That Friday night when she learned that Tony and Bob were double-dating with Denise and Judy again, she smiled and said, "Have a great time."

When Tony asked, "How about you? You got a date?" she nodded her head quickly and said, "No, but I'm going to be very busy watching *Count Dracula* on TV."

She was proud of herself because she actually had a good time that evening and didn't think much about Tony at all. *Maybe I'm finally becoming independent*, she congratulated herself.

Tony and Bob spent the next Saturday and Sunday working in the garage, and Maggie was even prouder of herself because she didn't find even one excuse to go out and join them. Absolutely determined that her new independence was going to be a permanent part of her personality, she called a girlfriend, and they went out on Saturday night to the roller-skating rink. On Sunday afternoon, she went for a long bicycle ride down along the lake and into the park. She had a happy day, and as she came home in time to prepare supper for the family, she scolded herself for having wasted the whole summer mooning over Tony when she could have been out having a good time.

That evening at supper, Tony complimented her on her marvelous chicken casserole and then said, "How about a game of Monopoly tonight, Maggie? I haven't seen much of you all week."

"No thanks," Maggie said airily. "I have to finish my English paper. It's the first one of the year, and I want to make sure I do a good job on it."

Tony looked a little surprised at Maggie's lighthearted refusal, and she thought that she detected a touch of disappointment as well. In the old days, her heart would have grabbed at any hint of interest on Tony's part, but now that she was the new, cool Maggie, she wasn't dependent on what Tony thought of her.

Maggie was in her room working on the report when her mother called her to the telephone. She was surprised to hear Jim's voice on the other end of the phone. Jim said, "Hi, Maggie. I thought we might try again. Want to go out with me tonight?"

"No," Maggie said, as definitely as she could. "I'm busy this evening."

"Well, how about tomorrow night?" Jim asked.

"I'll be busy then, too," Maggie said quickly.

"Tuesday?"

"Sorry."

"Wednesday?"

"No, Jim. I won't be able to go on Wednesday."

There was a long pause, and then Jim asked in a small voice, "Does this mean you don't want to go out with me at all?"

"I'm sorry, Jim," Maggie said firmly. "You were pretty crummy that Saturday night."

There was another long pause, then Jim said in a voice tinged with respect, "I'd like to call you again in a few weeks, if you don't mind, Maggie. See if you've changed your mind. Would that be all right?"

Maggie said that she didn't expect to change her mind, then she put the telephone down gently. She turned and almost bumped into Tony Angelo who had obviously been standing behind her listening to the whole conversation.

Maggie said, "Sorry," and started to duck away

from him, but Tony leaned forward and put his arm up against the wall so as to block her escape.

Although he wasn't actually touching her, his arms formed a kind of fence around her. Maggie was breathlessly aware that he was so close. He might as well have been touching her. She said uncertainly, "Hey, Tony. Let me go."

"I'm not holding you," Tony said. And then he smiled as though to say that it was a game. He asked, "Was that Hudson on the phone?"

"There *is* no Humphrey Hudson," Maggie explained patiently.

"Then who was it?" Tony asked.

Maggie started to tell him it was Jim. Then she shook her head. She said, "Tony, I'm not going to tell you who it is because it's really not for you to know. I don't mean to be rude, but Bob and Bruce are all the big brothers I can handle. I appreciate the fact that you're concerned about me, but I will have to get along without your advice from now on. I am growing up, and I'm more independent than you realize."

Tony wrinkled his forehead and seemed to think over what she had said to him. His expression was one of puzzlement, hurt, and curiosity. He said after a minute, "I guess you're telling me it's none of my business. Huh, Maggie?"

"Something like that," Maggie admitted.

Tony dropped one of his arms away from the wall, and Maggie turned to duck away from him. But Tony circled her waist with the arm that he had dropped and used the other arm to turn her chin upward and tilt her face toward his. He bent over and brushed her lips lightly with his own. Then he kissed her on the cheek and whispered in her ear, "Good-bye, Maggie. I guess you're all grown-up now. I'm going to miss you." With that, he turned and walked away from her.

Maggie stood in the hallway, her lips trembling from Tony's kiss, her cheek burning from his touch. Her feelings were a mixture of sadness and delight at his obvious recognition that she was, indeed, growing up. She whispered softly, "Good-bye, Tony. I love you." With that, she turned and went back to her room.

She knew now that she had finally broken through Tony's big-brother attitudes. She had convinced him she was an independent person. But it didn't feel as good as she'd hoped it would. It felt like a loss. Tony's kiss told her she'd hurt him terribly. He would never feel the same about her, and she would miss his warm concern. Though she was glad to have achieved her hard-won independence, she was dismayed and saddened by the loss of Tony's brotherly love.

She went to her room to begin work on her English paper. Suddenly, Maggie was frightened. For just one moment, she wished with all her heart that she could be a little girl again. But she knew it was too late.

From that moment on, Tony treated her with a new respect. He was friendly, but there was a distance and a coolness in their relationship that had simply never been there before. Maggie was sorry about that, but at the same time, she was glad that the respect was there.

It seemed to her that Bob's attitude changed at the same time that Tony's did. He acted more like Bruce. Though the teasing and the good times were gone, so were the bossiness and the nagging. The most ironic part of the whole situation was that just as Bob and Tony stopped nagging her about physical exercise, Maggie threw herself into sports again. She started taking long walks in the late afternoon. She enjoyed walking alone, and as far as she was concerned, the month of October was the most beautiful month in Massachusetts.

One Friday afternoon, she was walking home from school. Her shoes were slogging through a pile of red and yellow leaves. She felt the warm, October sun beating down on her light brown, shiny hair. The fall breeze made her shiver, and she hugged her deep green sweater tighter around her body. As she walked, the sky seemed to change from a crisp October day into the stormy, threatening sky of winter. Even though she knew it was too early, Maggie sniffed the air and was sure that she smelled snow. She jammed her mitten-less hands into her gray flannel trouser pockets and speeded up.

As she hurried toward her front door, the sky seemed to crack open, and heavy sheets of frosty rain that were half ice slashed through the sky. Maggie broke into a run and made a fast dash up the last two blocks to the Matthewses' house. She was breathing heavily, and her fingers and cheeks were numb with cold when she burst into the living room and called out, "Anybody home? It's miserable out there."

Bruce called from the kitchen, "Hi, Maggie. We're in here. Come meet Alan again."

Then Maggie remembered that this was the weekend that Bruce was bringing his college roommate home.

Maggie turned toward the kitchen, shivering like a wet puppy dog, and pulling off her sweater as she walked through the kitchen door, she called out, "Hi, Bruce. Hi, Alan. I'll be back in a minute. I got rained on."

Bruce was standing over the stove, waving a wooden spoon in one hand as he held a bowl of chopped onions in the other. He said, "Hope you don't mind if I cook tonight. I know it's your turn."

"I don't mind," Maggie said. "It just means less work for me. Did you have a good trip, Alan?" She turned to Bruce's roommate and smiled at him. She realized that he was standing up because she had entered the room. *What good manners he has*, Maggie thought. She was pleased he thought she deserved that sort of treatment.

In her most sophisticated voice, she murmured, "Please sit down. I'll be back in a moment." Then, turning, she went to her room where she dried her hair with a towel and pulled on her heaviest white wool turtleneck sweater to take away some of the chill. Her gray flannel trousers were soaked, so she changed into Levis and went back into the kitchen.

She was somewhat amused when she saw Alan

rise for a second time when she entered the kitchen. She turned to him and said, "Really, Alan, if you jump up every time I come into the room, you're going to get a lot of exercise this weekend. Sit down and forget about it."

Alan nodded his head and said, "You're right, of course. I'll try to remember." Then he sat down and looked at the plate of celery and onions that was in front of him.

Maggie pulled up a chair and asked, "Has Bruce got you doing all the hard work? Here, let me help you chop those." She took the knife from Alan and began chopping the celery and onions expertly. Turning to Bruce, she asked, "So how's college life, brother?"

"Just great," Bruce said, "but I got homesick for home cooking, so I came home."

"Don't you cook at school?" Maggie asked.

"Oh, yes, he does," Alan answered promptly. "Bruce is the best cook in our dormitory." And then he added, "And it's a coeducational dorm."

Bruce walked over to the table and picked up the chopped onions and celery, then turned and popped them into the skillet. As he stirred the sautéing vegetables, he explained, "I cook in the dorm, but it's not the same thing. We don't have the right pans, and half the time someone has drunk all the milk. It seems as though if you try to do anything more complicated than spaghetti, it's doomed to disaster."

"What are we having tonight?" Maggie asked.

"Spaghetti," Bruce answered, and they all laughed.

During the next hour, Maggie had a great time talking with Bruce and Alan about cooking, and listening to their stories about their first month at the university. Maggie decided that she liked Bruce's roommate, even though he had kind of formal, funny, old-fashioned manners.

All in all, he was quite a nice-looking young man, Maggie decided. His slender face seemed intelligent and sensitive, and she was pleased by the fact that he went to so much trouble to talk to her about her own interests, asking her questions about her school and what her hobbies were.

Maggie found herself describing the joys of long, solitary walks. After a rush of enthusiasm, she paused, flushed slightly, and said, "Tell me some more about your classes. Bruce says that you are in fine arts, but that you're really interested in making movies. Have you made any?"

Alan shook his head quickly and answered, "Only a couple of short, experimental things when I was in high school. And the pity of it all is that I won't be able to take any film courses for at least three semesters in school. They want you to take the old-fashioned design stuff first."

"But it all must be very interesting," Maggie said. "I love movies."

Bruce looked up from his spaghetti sauce and said, "I guess I should tell you, Alan, Maggie is our resident film critic. She knows movie actors and actresses the way some kids know the big-league ball-club team members. She's really quite a movie buff."

Alan raised one eyebrow in surprise and turned his body slightly toward Maggie as he asked, "Really? What sorts of movies do you like?"

"Oh, anything, really," Maggie answered, somewhat flustered to have her movie-watching taken seriously. For as long as she could remember, people had been making fun of her because she preferred John Wayne to any of the younger television actors.

"The films of John Huston?" Alan asked hopefully.

Maggie nodded her head and took a deep breath of relief as she said, "Oh, yes. I love *The Treasure of the Sierra Madre.*"

Alan's face broke into an open grin and he was obviously delighted. He said, "That's wonderful. So do I!" And with that he launched into a thirty-minute discourse on the great mythic values of the American western.

Maggie put her elbows on the table, propped her face up on her hands, and listened as Alan explained the finer points of John Huston's movies as opposed to Howard Hawks's movies. Then he went on to discuss neo-realism and the impact of the foreign films on American cinema.

When dinner was served, Alan was still talking about the impact of movies on American culture. At the evening meal, the whole Matthews family joined in the discussion, and Maggie was amused to find that her mother and father had seen many of the movies that she knew from television, when they were in high school. Somehow the idea of her mother and father holding hands as they watched Marilyn Monroe and Jane Russell in *Gentlemen Prefer Blondes* was more than Maggie could imagine.

Alan did most of the talking at dinner, and a couple of times Maggie thought that her father and mother seemed to shift slightly in their seats as though they were bored or restless. She wondered if they were tired of all of the conversation about movies.

After supper, Mr. and Mrs. Matthews seemed almost glad that it was their night to wash dishes. They left the three young people sitting around the dining room table talking, or to be more accurate, listening to Alan talk about movies, until seven-thirty. Then Bruce reminded his friend that they had dates. Alan looked absolutely dismayed at the thought. He turned to Maggie and said, "Will you join us?"

Maggie was amazed at the invitation, and she didn't really know exactly how to respond. She looked at Bruce, who lifted his shoulders in a slight shrug, as though to say, "Come along if you want to, but I think it would be a bit odd."

Maggie asked, "Don't you have dates?"

Alan dismissed the idea with some impatience and said, "We're picking up the two women you met the other night. But they wouldn't mind if a third person came along. Nobody really dates anymore," Alan said.

That was news to Maggie, and it appeared to be news to Bruce as well. He turned to his friend and asked, "Don't they?"

Alan looked rather supercilious as he said, "Well, not in the old-fashioned sense. I mean, taking June and Anne out bowling is hardly a Doris Day-Rock Hudson evening, would you say?"

Bruce grinned and said, "I would say, Alan, that if you measure all of reality by what you see in the movies, everything must seem very dull." Then he added, "But I think June is cuter than Doris Day."

The two young men seemed to have forgotten Maggie, who stood on the sidelines. She was still trying to decide whether to horn in on the party. When neither Alan or Bruce renewed the invitation, Maggie decided to drop the idea. After all, she couldn't expect them to want a sixteen-year-old to tag along, and she had plenty of things to do at home.

Nevertheless, spending the early part of the evening with them had been fun. It was interesting to talk to someone who thought of movies as a serious art form.

During the rest of that weekend, she spent a lot of time talking to Alan, and although he did seem to enjoy the sound of his voice too much, she developed quite a fondness for him. He was fun to be with, so when they went back to college on Sunday morning, she was sorry to see him go.

Alan pressed her hand firmly as he walked out the door and said to her, "I hope we see each other again very soon."

Maggie was pleased and thought again, *He really does have lovely manners.*

Seven

No one was more surprised than Maggie when the letter arrived from Alan the next Wednesday. Actually, there were two letters in the mailbox. Heavy, white stationery that obviously was expensive. In the upper left-hand corner was printed *A. Cooperman*, in dark gray.

Maggie handed her mother the letter addressed to Mr. and Mrs. Matthews and then said in a surprised voice, "Alan wrote a separate thank-you note to me. I wonder why he did that?"

Her mother, who was busy working on a column of figures, looked up absentmindedly and said, "Probably thought it would be the polite thing to do."

"Aren't you going to open yours?" Maggie asked.

Her mother put down her pencil and opened the thank-you note. She glanced at the handwritten note briefly and said, "Lovely manners; nice boy." Then she put the note aside.

Maggie, in the meantime, had been staring at her two-page letter with some bewilderment. The first page was about his schoolwork and an old movie he had seen the week before. The second page seemed to be an invitation to a football weekend at the university.

Maggie was surprised. Beyond that, she wasn't quite sure what she felt. She had not given any thought to the possibility that her brother's roommate might be interested in her except for the usual kid-sister interest she'd expected. Her voice betrayed some of that surprise when she said to her mother, "Alan wants me to come up to visit the university the weekend after this."

Her mother was busy on her bookwork again and nodded her head, saying, "That's nice. But we'll talk about it at dinner, Maggie."

Maggie left her mother's office with the feeling that Mrs. Matthews really hadn't understood the import of the invitation.

That evening at dinner, she brought up the subject again. She was secretly pleased with the surprise on Tony's and Bob's faces as she announced, "Alan Cooperman has invited me to be his date the weekend after this. He says I can stay in their dorm."

Mr. Matthews put down his fork and shook his head briefly, saying, "Out of the question. You're much too young to be spending the weekend in a coed dorm."

Maggie wasn't surprised at her father's reaction, but that didn't lessen her disappointment. She protested, "I'm sixteen years old. Lots of sixteen-year-olds date college men, don't they?"

She turned to Bob and Tony for some support. When both boys reluctantly nodded their heads in agreement, she went on. "Besides which, Bruce will be there. It's not as though you were letting me go to the farthest ends of the earth. The university is only forty miles away." She saw the firm look on her father's face — the one she thought of as his hard-line look — so she dropped her arguments.

When her mother said, "Let's talk about this later, shall we dear?" Maggie smiled gratefully. Long ago, Maggie had learned that if she pushed her father too far or insisted on an immediate answer, it would often be no. Better to let the subject drop and let him discuss it with her mother in private. It was very difficult for her father, she knew, to back down once he had made a firm statement. So she quickly turned the subject to the day's news.

Soon the Matthews family was engaged in a spirited discussion of whether or not school teachers and other public employees had the same right to strike as other workers.

If Tony was distressed or surprised by Maggie's invitation to the college, he didn't show it. Since her last encounter with him, Tony had been careful about what he said to her. In a way, Maggie missed the pleasure of exchanging brotherly conversation with him. In another way, she was glad to have their relations on a more formal basis. Maggie still thought about Tony a lot, but for the last two and a half weeks, she had made a conscious, successful effort to keep herself occupied with other things. All in all, Maggie felt very pleased with herself as she went to her room to study. Things were definitely better since she'd decided to stop being so obsessive about Tony.

Whether she was allowed to go to the college weekend or not, it was thrilling to have been invited. She enjoyed rereading Alan's letter several times during the next couple of days, and by the time there was another discussion about whether she would be allowed to go, she knew the letter by heart.

It was Saturday evening, and Bruce was home from college just for the day. Maggie was glad to see him and was hopeful that he would side with her in the inevitable family discussion. It was because she hoped for help from Bruce that she felt brave enough to bring up the subject again. That evening after supper, Bruce was clearing the table when Maggie asked, "Did you know that Alan invited me up to the university next weekend?"

A look of surprise flashed across Bruce's face and Maggie realized that he had not known it at all. Bruce shook his head quickly and said, "I wonder why he didn't tell me?"

Maggie wondered about that herself, and the answer that came to her mind was that Alan was ashamed of inviting a high school girl to be his date. Maggie asked, "Do you think he was afraid you'd disapprove?"

Bruce grinned that slow, thoughtful grin of his and Maggie noticed how much he looked like their father. He was growing his first beard, and the soft, red fuzz on his chin gave him a slightly disreputable air, but his bright blue eyes crinkled at the corners just the way her father's did. She realized that in another fifteen years he was going to be almost a carbon copy of Bruce Matthews, Sr.

Bruce said, "I'm not sure that I *do* approve, Maggie. You're still so young to me."

Maggie stiffened in preparation for the argument she was afraid was coming. She said quickly, "I'm only three years younger than you are, Bruce."

Bruce laughed and pointed out, "Three and three-quarters years, which is closer to four. Besides that, four years can make a big difference at our age, Maggie." Then he added in his usual thoughtful manner, "Of course, when I'm forty-four and you're forty, it won't make any difference. But right now you've got a lot of living to do, Maggie, before you're really grown-up." And then Bruce said under his voice, "For that matter, so does Alan Cooperman. He's only eighteen himself."

Somehow, Maggie resented Bruce's patronizing remarks about Alan even more than the remarks about herself. She felt a strong loyalty to Alan for having invited her to the dance. Had he damaged himself in Bruce's eyes because of that invitation? If so, she owed him something.

Maggie came quickly to his defense, saying, "I thought Alan was a very intelligent young man, and he has lovely manners."

"Oh, yes," Bruce answered. "I couldn't agree with you more." Then he was almost laughing as he added, "Of course, if you lived with him day in and day out the way I do, you might not be as impressed by all that brilliance and breeding. He certainly hasn't learned much in the way of the practical arts."

"Practical arts!" Maggie sneered. "You and Bob both think that anyone who can't handle a wrench or a hammer is an idiot. Alan Cooperman is an intellectual — not a mechanic."

"Yeah, right. Well, even intellectuals have to eat," Bruce said. "Alan can't cook or sew on a button or clean. He's got a long way to go." Bruce seemed to realize that he was being critical of his roommate, and he corrected himself, saying, "But that's not the point. You're not planning to marry him, are you, Maggie? You're only planning to come up and visit for the weekend." He smiled at his younger sister and drawled, "I think that will be a delightful experience. I always wanted to double-date with little Miss Mudpie."

As was often the case when dealing with her brothers, Maggie's reaction was a mixed one. She was angry at his patronizing tone of voice and at being called little Miss Mudpie. But she was grateful for his apparent offer of help. She smiled winsomely at her brother. "Then you'll talk to Dad?"

Bruce nodded his head and said, "I'll talk to Dad. Don't worry about it."

Maggie left Bruce in the kitchen, scrubbing pots and pans, and ran to her room to get her jacket. She was going with two friends to the movies and they would be at the house any minute.

By the time Maggie got home from the movies, it was all set. Her mother and father were playing chess in the kitchen. Bruce was looking on, giving a running commentary. When Maggie went to the refrigerator to pour herself a glass of milk to have with the leftover brownies, her mother looked up from the chess game and said, "Bruce has just convinced us that you should be allowed to go for the weekend."

Her father added his admonitions along with his permission. "But remember, permission to go to college is not permission to behave like a college student. No drinking, and nothing we wouldn't let you do at home. Bruce has promised that he will take good care of you. We're counting on his good sense." As an afterthought, her father added, "And your own."

Maggie reassured them. She said, "Alan is a perfectly truthworthy person, Daddy, and so am I."

Her father looked as though he would like to argue with that, but instead he just clamped his mouth shut in a tight line and went back to the chess game.

Maggie was still eating brownies and watching the chess game when Tony and Bob came in from their dates. Tony was spending the night at the Matthewes' house because he and Bob were getting up early in the morning to go on their first hunting trip of the season.

Both Bob and Tony had deer rifles and licenses, but Maggie knew that neither of the boys relished the idea of shooting anything. It was a family joke that they were capable of tramping through the woods for hours and coming home with nothing but wild flowers or nuts they'd gathered. In fact, when they came in, Mr. Matthews looked up from his chess game long enough to say, "You boys are going nut-gathering tomorrow, I understand."

Bob flushed, and Maggie realized that he was reacting the same way she often did to an older person's patronizing tone. Bob said, "We're going to try the Hudson property this year. A fellow at school said hunting's a lot better over there."

"Terrible sport!" Maggie said to no one in particular. "All those people running around in their orange jackets shooting at poor little deer. I can't imagine anything worse than killing one." She shuddered at the thought.

Tony grinned at her and said, "Your problem is you saw *Bambi* at too early an age. Hunting deer is nothing like you imagine. Want to come along tomorrow?"

"Certainly not!" Maggie rejoined, although she was pleased at the invitation. "I wouldn't kill a rabbit, let alone a deer," Maggie said.

"But you do kill mosquitoes," Bob pointed out reasonably.

"Everyone kills mosquitoes."

"It's really only a question of degree," Bob insisted. "Mosquitoes, rabbits, or deer — what's the difference? If you were a Jain Hindu, you would walk with your eyes to the ground so you could avoid killing even the bugs in the earth."

Maggie replied, "And if you kill deer, why not kill cows or horses? It's all sport, isn't it?" She turned to her brother Bruce and said in a disdainful voice, "I'm sure no one at the university is a hunter. Tell them, Bruce."

Bruce looked a little surprised and answered, "As far as I know, there are more people against hunting than for hunting, but don't be too sure that everyone in college is going to agree with every one of your opinions, Maggie. College isn't like that. Different strokes for different folks, you know."

"When I get there next weekend," Maggie announced, "I'm going to take an informal poll. I'll bet you that I don't find one person on that campus who's in favor of shooting defenseless creatures."

Mrs. Matthews, having just won the chess game, stood up, stretched her arms overhead in a large yawn and smiled at her children. "It seems as though this is the most pointless argument you've had all week," she said to Maggie. "Neither Tony nor Bob has ever shot anything, except a couple of old tin cans. If they want to go tramping through the woods in orange jackets, let them do it. The outdoors is good for them."

Although Maggie was sure that her mother was essentially correct, she hated to let the argument go. In a way, she realized that arguing with Tony was just about the only contact she was having with him these days. As she sat on the wooden stool with her back against the refrigerator, she tipped back on two legs and turned her body slightly away from her mother to look more closely at Tony's face.

Tony had apparently lost interest in the conversation and was picking up the newspaper, rifling toward the back where Maggie knew he would read the comics. One of the most endearing things about Tony was the way he could find simple things to give him such pleasure. He loved comics. He loved the children's shows on television. He loved small children and animals, and it was part of what made him such a lovable person himself.

As Tony bent his head to read, the overhead kitchen light struck his dark brown, curly hair, making it seem as though there were a halo of gold around his head. The light pointed up the shadows on his face, and Maggie secretly admired his beautiful, straight nose and high, wide cheekbones. His dark eyelashes were dropped over his cheeks, and she looked down at the double-fringed eyelashes and his heavy, dark, straight brows that seemed like wings of color across his face. Tony was, in her opinion, one of the best-looking men that she had ever seen.

She couldn't help mentally comparing him to Alan Cooperman. She shook her head. *Tony's the boy for me*, she thought, and sighed aloud.

Her mother looked up and said, "I think it's

everyone's bedtime. Maggie, you too. You look tired."

Sometimes when her mother offered advice of this sort, Maggie argued with her, but this evening she nodded her head and agreed. Slipping off the stool, she kissed her mother and father on the cheek to say good night and then impulsively kissed Bob and Bruce. At which point, Tony looked up from the comics and asked in a petulant voice, "How about me?"

Maggie surprised herself and everyone else by walking over to the place where Tony sat and throwing her arms around his shoulders. Then she bent her head and kissed Tony fully on the mouth. The kiss she gave Tony was longer and stronger than any of the other kisses she had given that evening.

Tony seemed taken aback as she pulled her head away from him. For one brief second, he looked into her eyes, and there was a question in his own dark brown eyes.

Maggie thought she saw something else in Tony's eyes. Was it a flicker of interest? Perhaps. But then, to cover her own embarrassment at her forwardness, and to bring the incident back to normalcy, she grinned and pulled a lock of his hair, saying lightly, "That'll teach you!"

Everyone laughed except Tony. Tony was still looking at her with those deep brown, velvet eyes. Maggie was caught by his gaze. She wanted to tell the truth to him. She would have given anything in the world to bend over and kiss his lips one more time, but of course, she didn't. She just couldn't tell Tony how much she felt for him.

Pretending exhaustion, she turned and left the room. Behind her she could hear the soft murmurs of conversation in the kitchen. No doubt they were talking about tomorrow. *Well, let them talk,* thought Maggie. *Tonight is my special event. Tonight I kissed my love.* Humming to herself, she went to the bathroom to brush her teeth and get ready for bed.

Eight

Riding up to Northampton on the Greyhound bus was fun. Maggie had never traveled anywhere on her own before, and she enjoyed talking to the bus driver, who pointed out the sights along the way.

Despite her father's warning and her mother's added cautions, Maggie was not the least bit nervous about traveling alone. As the bus twisted through the New England villages, Maggie enjoyed every minute of looking at the white clapboard houses and the old, brick churches. There were still red and gold leaves clinging to a few trees as they went through the Berkshire Mountains.

About four-thirty, a big wind came up and Maggie knew that that was the end of the glorious fall foliage. She watched the wind pelt the red leaves to the ground, with some sadness. Shivering in her down jacket, Maggie hugged herself and stared out the window of the bus. For some reason, watching the wind and dark skies made her think of Tony. What was Tony doing this weekend? Was he going out with Denise again?

Maggie sat up straight and fished around in the brown bag that her mother had sent with her. She found the cheese sandwiches and the apple and raisins that her mother called "a little snack." Biting into the crisp, red apple, Maggie deliberately forced her thoughts away from Tony and back to the anticipation of the weekend that was before her. It was her first college weekend, and she was not going to let thoughts about Tony Angelo spoil it for her.

Maggie was surprised and pleased when Alan met her at the bus station without Bruce. Somehow, she'd expected that Bruce would be there, too. Perhaps because she knew that she would never be *really* interested in Alan, she wasn't very nervous. She greeted him with pleasure and no self-consciousness. When he insisted on carrying her suitcase, she let him. Alan couldn't be anything other than formally courteous, so she might as well relax and enjoy being his guest.

Alan didn't have a car, but he had borrowed Bruce's to pick her up. As they drove to the college campus, Alan pointed out the sights along the way and told her some of the local history, pointing to the lovely, brick buildings covered with ivy. "There are a lot of colleges in this area," he said. "The university is the biggest and has the newest buildings. It doesn't have the charm of some of the smaller schools like Smith or Hampshire, but I like it. And it has a good art department."

"It's pretty up here," Maggie said happily as she snuggled into her jacket. The November wind whipped through the cracks of Bruce's old automobile, and Maggie wished she had brought a heavy wool sweater to wear under her gray flannel blazer.

Alan asked, "Are you cold?"

"A little," she admitted. And for a moment she wondered if Alan would behave like Jim. Was he going to use her admission as an excuse to put his arm around her shoulder? Maggie hoped not.

Alan merely said, "We're almost there," and kept right on talking about the colleges and town.

Bruce seemed glad to see her when she walked in the door, but Maggie was relieved that he didn't make a big thing of it. He introduced her to two of their floor-mates, Shirley and Alice, and the five of them grabbed a quick supper of toasted cheese sandwiches and Cokes before going on the tour of the campus that Bruce had promised.

Bruce drove, and Maggie sat in the front seat until they picked up Bruce's date, Patty Anne, at her dormitory. After that, Maggie sat in the back seat with Alan. Suddenly, she felt a little nervous about being with Alan, but she decided the weekend really wasn't going to be a problem at all. Alan talked a lot. In fact, he talked so much that Maggie discovered all she had to do was nod her head occasionally and smile pleasantly.

Bruce and Patty Anne didn't seem to be listening much to the conversation in the backseat, and Maggie was glad. She sat back and enjoyed the drive through the college campus. Then Bruce parked the car in front of the big, old library and said, "It's really too dark to see much. Would you like to walk through our library?"

Maggie quickly agreed. She was glad to get out of the car and stretch her legs after her long afternoon bus ride. They climbed the steep stairs to the first floor of the library. Alan, Bruce, and Patty Anne pointed out various features including the periodical reading room and the large circulation desk.

"I have a pass to the film section," Alan said proudly. "Professor Adamson arranged it for me the second week I was in his class. I'm the only freshman in the school with a pass."

Maggie turned to Alan and tried to look suitably impressed. "That's great, Alan."

Alan's face lit up in an excited smile, and he said, "Would you like to take a look at some of the old silent films we have on file, Maggie? We've got one of the original copies of *Potemkin*."

Maggie didn't have any idea who or what or when *Potemkin* was, and she would have liked to have asked. But she was committed to an aura of sophistication, so she only nodded her head slightly, indicating mild interest.

"Great!" Alan said, and his eyes were shining brightly. He pointed toward a doorway over on the right. He said, "We can spend the whole evening there if you like."

Bruce frowned and shook his head, saying,

"Alan, we promised we would go to Lester's party. Don't you remember? There's bluegrass music and contra-dancing."

"Maggie wouldn't be impressed with contra-dancing," Alan said. "She's far too intellectual for that, aren't you, Maggie?"

Maggie stood in the middle of the two young men and looked from one to the other. What should she say? How should she answer? The truth was she was dying to try out contra-dancing. Ever since Bruce described the wonderful new folk dances he was learning at college, she'd wanted to see them, and she loved bluegrass music. But if she admitted that to Alan, wouldn't she look young in his eyes? She really didn't know what to say.

But finally, because she could no longer stand the silence, Maggie took a deep breath and said, "I'd love to see the movies if that's all right with you, Bruce."

Her older brother shrugged his shoulders and said, "I didn't have any idea you were interested in silent films."

Neither did I, Maggie thought, but she didn't have to say anything out loud because Alan broke in with an impatient, "Of course she is!" He took Maggie by the hand, saying to Bruce and Patty Anne, "We'll walk home when the library closes."

Patty Anne seemed to sense some of Maggie's difficulties in making up her mind, because she suggested, "Why don't you walk over to the party after the library closes? That way, Maggie could have a taste of both worlds."

114

Maggie looked gratefully at the older girl and said, "That would be wonderful! Could we do that, Alan?"

Alan seemed slightly put out at the suggestion, but he did not argue. "If you want to," he answered, "but let's hurry or we won't get to see all of *Potemkin*, and I'd like to show you some of the other early Eisenstein flicks. I'll bet you're crazy about Eisenstein, aren't you?"

"Sure I am," Maggie answered gravely, and her brother Bruce looked at her, raised one eyebrow, and whistled softly through his teeth.

Alan wasn't looking at Bruce, so Maggie was able to ignore her brother's obvious disapproval. She turned and walked with Alan toward the film library after saying good-bye to Bruce and Patty Anne.

Alan was so eager to show her the old Russian silent movies that it was no problem at all for her to cover up the fact that she had no idea who Eisenstein was or what *Potemkin* was. He seemed especially pleased by the fact that his library had the film recorded at the original silent movie speed. He spent a long time explaining that it eliminated the jerky, bouncy rhythm of most silent movies she would have seen on television.

Although Maggie spent a lot of time watching old movies, she'd never seen any silent films at all except for short clips of Charlie Chaplin and Laurel and Hardy. She had no idea what to expect as she sat down in the small, dark room and watched Alan insert the videotape into the movie viewing booth.

The room itself was about the size of the pantry off the kitchen at home. At first, she was uncomfortable sitting alone with Alan. *Will he try to kiss me?* she wondered. But she soon realized that while the movies were going on, Alan was much too enthusiastic about the films to pay any attention to her at all.

Maggie watched the dark black-and-white silent film as carefully as she could, listening to Alan's comments about Eisenstein's film techniques. At first, Maggie had no interest in the images flashing across the screen, but then she began to focus her mind on the movie. By the time the film got to the part where the people were being slaughtered on the streets of Moscow by the Czar's soldiers, Maggie's hands were gripping the sides of the chair with excitement. She was fully captivated by the movie. When it drew to a close, she turned to Alan and said in a voice of genuine enthusiasm, "That was absolutely wonderful!"

Alan seemed extremely pleased that she was impressed, and he answered, "Wait until you see *Alexander Nevsky.* It's a much better film technically. Now when we are watching that, pay special attention to the light and dark shadows and the way Eisenstein uses crowds. His was seminal work in the field of films. No serious film student can do anything until he or she studies Eisenstein's work. You might say he's the Shakespeare of film literature. Don't you agree, Maggie?"

Maggie had absolutely no idea what Alan was talking about, but she said quietly, "Of course."

Then she settled back in the chair to watch the beginning of her second silent movie.

They saw two-thirds of that before the attendant knocked on the door. "Library closes at ten on Friday night," he said.

Alan rewound the film, and they walked out of the library, down the long steps to the street. It was a cold November night. Maggie pulled her jacket closer around her shoulders and said to Alan, "I really loved *Potemkin*." She did not tell him that she found *Alexander Nevsky* absolutely incomprehensible. He was so busy talking about Eisenstein's techniques that he did not notice her omission. They were walking quickly now because the air was so cold. Even so, Maggie shivered and Alan slipped his arm around her shoulder. She looked up at him and said, "Let's run. We'll get to the dance faster."

Alan frowned and asked, "Do you really want to go to that silly dance? Let's go back to the dorm and I'll show you my collection of film books. You'd like that better, wouldn't you?"

Maggie didn't see how she could say anything but yes. They were inside the dorm, sitting in the living room, when Bruce came home at one o'clock in the morning. Bruce didn't look very pleased that Maggie was sitting on the couch looking at film books while Alan sat with his arm around her.

Maggie knew immediately that Bruce was ready to take a superior, big-brother attitude toward her. She decided to counter his criticism by speaking before he had a chance to say anything.

Though she honestly found Alan boring, she was flattered by all the attention he was paying her. She certainly didn't have any intention of letting her brother spoil the weekend for her.

"Oh, we had a wonderful time," she said to Bruce quickly. "Do you know that Alan has almost thirty books on film right here in this dorm?"

"Yes, I know it," Bruce answered shortly. "You missed a good dance."

"Maggie doesn't care for dances," Alan said. "She's too intellectual for that kind of nonsense."

Bruce raised one eyebrow and looked at his younger sister. Maggie held her breath. What was Bruce going to say? But all Bruce did was repeat the one word, "Intellectual?" with a question mark at the end. Then he suggested, "How about if we all go to bed now? We've got a big day ahead of us tomorrow. We're going to Patty Anne's for breakfast and then there's the football game and the dance tomorrow evening. You don't want to be worn out for the dance, do you, Cinderella?"

Maggie smiled gratefully at her brother and followed him to the room where she was supposed to sleep. The dorm had seven bedrooms and a common living room and kitchen. Maggie would be using the room of a boy who was visiting his parents in Iowa.

Never in her life had she seen such a messy collection of books, papers, and clothes, piled in corners. Maggie looked around the room and imagined what her mother would say if she saw her darling daughter sleeping in such disarray. Bruce said, "I'm sorry about this, Maggie. I changed the sheets, but I really couldn't do more than that. Each of us has our own way of house-keeping, and since we all have to live together, we try to stay out of each other's hair." Then he grinned and said, "They call me 'The Neatener' because I'm so much fussier than they are."

Maggie said, "It won't bother me, Bruce. I'll be perfectly comfortable here." But privately, she wondered why anyone would choose to live like that.

Within fifteen minutes she was sound asleep and dreaming — not about college campuses or *Potemkin* — but dreaming the same old dream about Tony Angelo.

She woke in the morning and the first thing she thought about was Tony. As she brushed her teeth and combed her hair it was Tony who was on her mind. What was he doing on this Saturday morning? Would he be coming over to the Matthewses' house soon? Were he and Bob going to be working on cars in the garage?

Maggie smiled at her reflection in the mirror. She was frightened at the difference between what Alan thought she was like and what she was really like. She could tell from the way Alan talked to her last night that he thought she was an intel-lectual. She knew she was really an ordinary sixteen-year-old girl with a crush on an ordinary eighteen-year-old boy.

Alan was the farthest thing from what she wanted in a boy. He talked too much. And his conversation was only about himself and his own interests. Though he was nice enough, Maggie knew he was wrong for her. The things she wanted in a boy were warmth and humor and fun — all the things Tony had.

Then, Maggie promised herself she would be very careful not to let her thoughts of home and Tony get in the way of enjoying this experience. She went through the day with pleasure and interest, but she did not find herself as enthusiastic about it as she might have guessed. Obviously, Bruce expected her to be more impressed than she was. She liked the college and the people she met, but it wasn't really as glamorous or exciting as she'd expected. Bruce was right when he'd warned her that many of his classmates seemed younger than she was. The longer she was with Alan, the more she understood that he didn't see her at all. What he saw was an image of a girl he would like to know. He paid her a lot of compliments, and that was nice, but Maggie knew the compliments were based on Alan's fantasies. He talked a lot about how bright she was. Maggie knew that she was smart enough, but nothing like Alan seemed to want to believe.

That night at the dance, she tried to tell him who she really was. They were sitting on the sidelines watching Bruce and Patty Anne and the other couples dancing to an old 1930's tango tune. Maggie was disappointed when Alan admitted he didn't know how to dance at all. He went on to say that Maggie was so intellectual he knew she really wouldn't care. Now she was on her third Coke and gazing wistfully at the couples on the floor. Alan was on his second hour of conversation about movies. He was talking about how the American movie industry had changed when the foreign films such as *The Bicycle Thief* came to American shores after World War II. Maggie, covering a yawn with a forced smile, interrupted long enough to stand up and say, "Excuse me, Alan, I'll be right back."

Alan stopped in mid-sentence and looked surprised. He asked, "Would you like me to see if I can find someone to dance with you?"

"Oh, would you?" Maggie asked enthusiastically. "I'd love that!"

Alan said, "I guess you think it's funny for me to have invited you to a dance if I wasn't going to dance, don't you?"

Maggie smiled in a manner that she hoped was cheerful. "I would like to dance," she admitted.

When she got back from the ladies' room, Alan explained, "I invited you to the dance because I wanted to get to know you better. That weekend at your home, I saw that you were an extremely perceptive and wonderful person. I hope we can be very good friends, Maggie." He took her hand in his and ran his fingers lightly over her palm.

Maggie let him keep her hand, but answered evasively, "You may not be as interested in me when you get to know me better, Alan. I'm really nothing like what you think I am."

Alan squeezed her hand. "Oh, yes, you are. I know exactly who you are, Margaret Matthews, and you're the girl for me."

She told herself that Alan would change his mind once she went home. When a friend of Alan's came over and asked her to dance, she accepted gratefully. Maggie danced twice with him and once with Bruce. By the time the evening was over, she was so bored that she was honestly glad to get home.

As they walked into the dorm, she turned to Alan and said, "Thank you. I had a nice time."

He offered, "Would you like to see that biography of Chaplin I was telling you about?"

Maggie shook her head gently and said, "Not tonight, Alan. I'm really very tired, and my bus goes back to the city early in the morning."

He bent over to kiss her good night. Maggie would have let him kiss her. After all, it was her first date on a college campus and she would have felt very silly protesting. But Bruce walked from the kitchen back into the living room just as Alan bent to kiss her on the lips. Maggie felt awkward, so she turned her head to the side. Alan's kiss landed on her cheek and she was happy enough about that.

"Good night," she said. "It was a wonderful weekend."

"Oh, I'll see you off to the bus tomorrow," Alan protested.

"I've decided to take the 6:30 A.M. bus," Maggie said. "I have some work I have to do before school on Monday."

"I'll set the alarm," Alan said firmly.

"Well, if you really want to," Maggie answered, "but you don't have to. You've been a charming and wonderful date."

Maggie hoped that the word "charming" would lend the right touch to what she wanted to say. By now she was absolutely convinced that she never wanted to go out with Alan again. She would rather stay home than hear another word about old movies. In fact, when she got home, she had just about decided that she would give up watching old movies altogether — at least for a little while.

Nine

On Monday morning, on the way to school, Tony asked her perfunctorily, "Have a nice time?" She said yes, and Bob and Tony went on with their usual conversation. Maggie sat in the backseat feeling just as misplaced and out of things as before.

On the way home from school that evening, she tried to bring up the subject of her weekend date by saying, "Do you see that ivy over there on that lawn? The university is totally covered with that sort of ivy."

"That so?" Tony asked, and it was clear from the tone of his voice that he was not interested in ivy.

"It was a beautiful school," Maggie ventured another time.

"Too big," Tony said.

"Too big," Bob agreed. "I'm going to a small school."

"Me, too," Tony added.

"I think you should at least check out the university," Maggie said. "It's not good to have such closed minds at your age."

She hoped her criticism would interest them if nothing else did, but Tony and Bob seemed immune. They went back to their conversation about mechanics. Maggie reminded herself of her promise not to let herself get hung up on Tony's lack of interest in her.

As they pulled into the driveway, Maggie said, "I think it's going to snow today."

Tony looked up at the sky, shook his head, and said, "You're crazy." With that, he opened the car door for himself and walked straight into the garage.

Maggie sat for a moment in the back of the car, trying to get control of her emotions. These days it seemed as though she was so moody — she was down one moment and up the next — and she hated it. She longed for the good old days when she had been plain old cheerful Maggie Matthews. She wanted to be twelve years old again. But even as she was thinking these solemn thoughts, she knew they weren't true. Maybe it would be better when she was eighteen years old. *Yes*, she thought, *eighteen must be easier than this*. But even as she was thinking this, she was remembering that Patty Anne, Bruce, and Alan didn't seem to have it all together either. *Maybe there's never a perfect time*, Maggie told herself. And somehow the possibility of that made her happier. If this was what life was like, she could probably get used to it.

125

Maggie's moods swung between hope and depression for the rest of the afternoon and evening. One minute she'd chatter and sound wonderful, the next minute she'd be down in the dumps. At dinner, her parents pointedly avoided commenting on her moodiness, and after a few polite questions about her college weekend, they dropped that subject as well.

As Maggie pushed peas around her bright blue plate, she tried to remember the last time she'd been really happy. Was it when she'd taken the bicycle ride with Tony? Thinking about the bicycle ride with Tony made her remember the warm kiss they'd shared.

"Maggie, you're not listening again." Her mother broke in on her thoughts. "It seems to me you spend so much time staring into space. Whatever in the world do you think about?"

Maggie answered quickly, "I was thinking about my history project. I don't know whether to write about Jane Addams or Abigail Adams. What do you think?"

"Take Abigail Adams," her mother said. "It was an interesting period in history. And Abigail Adams was an extraordinary woman."

"So was Jane Addams," her father disagreed. "After all . . ."

The conversation bounced back and forth between her parents, and Maggie was happy that she'd found a way to distract their attention. It was depressing enough to be herself without having both her parents worried over her.

They were still discussing the respective merits of the two women when the telephone rang and her brother Bob answered it. He came out looking slightly surprised as he said, "Maggie, it's long distance for you. Person-to-person."

Maggie went to the telephone feeling confused about who it might be. She was amazed when she heard, "Hello, Maggie. It's Alan. I wanted to make sure that I got you. I thought you might be out on a date."

"No," Maggie said. Then she waited. What did Alan want?

"I called to tell you I had a lovely time and I hope you can come up again soon."

"That would be nice," Maggie said.

"Do you think you might come up next weekend?" Alan said.

"Oh, no," Maggie said quickly. "My parents would never allow that." She didn't add that she had no intention of asking her parents. She was sure she didn't want to encourage Alan. At the same time, she was pleased that Alan thought enough about her to ask.

He seemed disappointed as he said, "Well, maybe you can come the weekend after that. I'll call again and we can talk about it later. I was sorry that you didn't get to see my biography of Charlie Chaplin. Would you like me to send it to you in the mail? You could mail it back."

She said quickly, "I'll check in the library and see if they have it there."

There was a long pause, and Maggie didn't

know what else to say. Finally, Alan said, "Well, I was just thinking about you and so I thought I'd call you up and see how you are."

"I'm fine," Maggie said. Again, there was a long pause. Then she said, "Alan, you'd better hang up now. This call is costing you a fortune."

"I suppose so," Alan said, "but I called person-to-person so I'd be sure and get you. You don't have a date tonight, do you, Maggie?"

Maggie's mind raced as she tried to decide how to answer Alan. Finally it seemed the best thing to do was tell him the truth. "I'm not allowed to date on week nights," she said. "My parents are very strict."

Alan laughed lightly and said in an amused voice, "It's always so hard for me to remember that you're only sixteen. You're so intelligent and sensitive. But then, age is really relative, isn't it?"

"Alan, you'd better hang up now," Maggie said. He was really making her uncomfortable.

"All right, my dear," he replied, "but I'll call you again soon. May I?"

"Why, yes," Maggie answered, not knowing what else to say.

She hung up the phone and walked back to the dinner table where her family waited expectantly. "That was Alan," she said. "He wanted me to come up to the college again."

Before her parents had a chance to object, she continued, "I told him I couldn't. At least not right away."

Her mother smiled and said, "Seems you're

turning into quite a *femme fatale*, but don't let it go to your head, Maggie. School's the most important thing in your life right now — not boys."

"You're right," Maggie answered, with a quick nod of the head. She had no intention of arguing with her parents about a boy she wasn't even interested in. Now if *Tony* should ask her out on a school night, that was worth fighting for. But Tony was not going to ask her out. Besides that, her folks probably would never object to her going out with Tony. They thought of him as a sort of adopted son.

She was pleased by the way she'd handled the conversation with Alan. She'd been honest, and that felt a lot better than lying. In general, Maggie was feeling better and better about herself.

Ten

Tony was there when the flowers arrived. It was Saturday afternoon, and Maggie was up in her room reading a book about Abigail Adams. She heard the doorbell ring, but decided to let Bob answer it. She was very surprised to hear Tony call out, "Hey, Maggie, it's for you."

Closing the book, Maggie went to the living room, where Tony was holding a basket of chrysanthemums. He held them out to her, saying, "Your boyfriend sent these."

Maggie knew immediately that the flowers were from Alan. She looked down at the lovely orange and gold balls of color. The flowers were really very lovely. They were the first flowers she'd ever received and they made her feel special.

She was happy as she smiled and asked Tony, "Aren't they lovely?"

Tony frowned and said in a voice that was visibly distressed, "What's that creep sending you flowers for?"

Maggie quickly defended Alan, saying, "He's not a creep. He's a very nice person."

"He has to be a creep," Tony said shortly. "Anyone who'd send flowers to a girl he's only been out with once is a creep."

"You don't appreciate civilized people," Maggie retorted quickly. "Your problem is you've spent so many years in a dark and damp garage, you've turned into a troll. The more I see you, the more you remind me of a creature from the black garage." Maggie realized she was being too hard on Tony, but she'd be darned if she was going to let him or anyone else spoil the pleasure of receiving her first flowers. She held the basket out and said, "Come on, admit it. They're beautiful, aren't they? And they smell wonderful."

Tony protested, "They look all right, but chrysanthemums smell funny." Deciding that arguing with Tony was going to get her nowhere, Maggie carried the flowers straight back to her bedroom, where she put them on her desk.

That afternoon, as she worked on the Adams report, she enjoyed looking at the fall chrysanthemums. But the flowers didn't change her opinion of Alan. If anything, they worried her. Were the flowers an indication of the trouble she was going to have discouraging him?

That evening when Alan called, she said to her mother, "Please tell him I'm not home."

"But you are home," Mrs. Matthews said impatiently. "Besides, how do you know it's Alan? Maybe it will be someone else. You answer the phone. I'm busy."

"It's Alan," Maggie said, but she lifted the receiver on the fourth ring.

Sure enough, it was Alan, who began the conversation by imitating Humphrey Bogart in *Casablanca*.

Maggie didn't even pretend to think that it was funny. Instead, she said, "Oh, Alan, don't call me every night. My folks are really getting upset about this."

"But a beautiful woman like you will always have lots of suitors," Alan said gallantly. "Your folks will just have to adjust to that fact. I was sitting here watching Cyd Charisse on television, thinking of you. Do you know that you look a little like her?"

Maggie laughed at the idea that she looked anything at all like the dark, beautiful dancer. She said, "Alan, you really are crazy. You know that? I don't look a thing like Cyd Charisse."

"Oh, yes," Alan answered promptly. "You've got long, glorious legs and a wonderful smile, just like hers. I wish you were here with me this evening. Maggie, I'm going to try to talk Bruce into bringing me home to visit next weekend. Will you be free?"

Inwardly Maggie groaned. She didn't really want to spend another weekend with Alan Cooperman. She said, "No. Not next weekend. Next weekend I'm going on a three-day camping trip with some friends." It was a lie, and she thought that Alan probably would know it was, but she didn't care. His attention was making her feel uncomfortable and foolish. She wished he would take the hint and leave her alone. But Alan seemed more interested in talking than in listening, and it was another five minutes before she hung up the telephone.

Sunday night when he called, she tried again to get her mother to say she wasn't home. Her mother shook her head and said firmly, "Maggie, if you're not interested in the boy, you're going to have to tell him. I can't spend my life fending off romantic young men for you. It's part of growing up beautiful, you know, having these boys call you like this."

"Oh, Mother, I'm not beautiful. Alan's just imagining it. There's nothing beautiful about me at all, and I don't want to talk about him on the telephone. He thinks I'm Bette Davis or someone. It's just so weird. I can't even explain to you how strange it is."

"Alan's a nice boy and you're a lovely girl," her mother said. "If you don't want to see him anymore, that's your choice. But you're going to have to learn to handle these things yourself."

By this time the telephone had rung ten times. Maggie walked as slowly as she could to answer it. Perhaps if she pretended she was wounded in her right foot, she could slow her progress down enough to keep from having to talk to Alan again tonight. But, no matter how slowly Maggie walked, that day and the days following, Alan kept the phone ringing. Each night at exactly seven o'clock, Maggie had a conversation with her self-appointed true love.

As the week went on, the conversations seemed to Maggie to get farther and farther away from reality. She would say, "Alan, I'm really not interested in having a romance with you."

He would say, "It's all right if you don't love me, Maggie. I have enough love for both of us. In time you'll grow to care."

Maggie recognized that much of his dialogue came from old movies, and she began to wonder if Alan was quite right in the head.

Maggie couldn't help but notice that Tony was arranging his life so that he was in the Matthewses' living room every night at seven. Was it possible that Alan's attentions were actually getting the reaction from Tony that she'd tried so hard for earlier? Maggie tried not to think about it too much. She was determined not to spend her life daydreaming about Tony.

Even so, she couldn't help but notice the way he watched her when she walked across the living room floor. It was impossible to ignore the way their hands touched when they did dishes together. In a hundred little ways she was aware of a certain electricity that was snapping during these evenings. She didn't really trust her perceptions, though. It seemed as though she'd lived with a fantasy about Tony for so long. Perhaps the most important way Tony had changed was that he always seemed to be around. Maggie enjoyed his company in a very new and different way.

It was three weeks after Maggie had gone to the university before anything really important happened between them. It was early afternoon, and she was sitting at the kitchen table. She'd left school early to go to the dentist and was home when Tony and Bob came in.

Bob asked Tony, "Are you sure you don't want to come with me?"

Tony shook his head, saying slowly, "I'll stay here and help Maggie with her homework."

"Okay," Bob said. "I'll be back in about an hour. But I don't know why you don't want to come with me. It's a nice day out."

Again, Tony shook his head and drawled, "No, I'll just stay here and keep Maggie company."

Maggie sucked in her breath and tried to keep her heart from pounding as she realized that it was finally happening. For the first time, Tony was making an obvious choice to spend time with her.

When Bob left, Tony pulled up a chair beside Maggie and said in a soft voice, "I hope I'm not keeping you from anything important."

Maggie smiled and tried to keep her voice calm as she answered, "Of course not. I've got another whole week on this Adams project. I'm practically finished."

Tony nodded his head in approval, saying, "You always were a good student, Maggie. I think that's great!"

Maggie blushed a little bit and managed to say, "Thank you."

Tony reached over and touched one of the chrysanthemums sitting on the kitchen table. He asked casually, "Did your boyfriend send you these?"

Quickly, Maggie shook her head and answered, "He's not my boyfriend."

Letting that go, Tony pursued, "But he did send these, didn't he?"

Remembering what kind of trouble she'd gotten into before because of her lies to Tony, she told the truth. "No, Alan didn't send these," Maggie said. "Mom bought them at the grocery store yesterday. Thy're pretty, aren't they?"

Tony reached over and broke a yellow chrysanthemum from its stem, then reached toward Maggie, holding the flower in his hand. Maggie's heart began to beat faster as she realized Tony was about to touch her. She held her breath as he tucked the bright yellow flower into her hair. It rested over her ear. Then he smiled at her and said, "You should wear flowers all the time, Maggie. It suits you."

Maggie didn't know what to say. She was stunned by the obviously romantic comment. Was she imagining things or was Tony looking at her in an entirely different way? The sunlight streamed in on the kitchen, breaking over the dining room table, shining onto the flowers, and reflecting the warmth and the beauty of the day.

Tony took his hand away from the flower and dropped it along her chinline, tracing his finger beneath her jaw to the tip of her chin. Maggie held her breath as Tony leaned forward to kiss her tenderly on the lips.

The kiss seemed longer and stronger than any kiss she had ever had. Whether the kiss lasted ten seconds or ten minutes, Maggie wasn't sure.

For a while it seemed as though time was truly standing still.

When she finally broke the kiss and leaned back, she sighed softly and smiled up at him. He said in a quiet voice, "You're really quite a girl, aren't you, Maggie? You've grown up."

Maggie tried to laugh as she said, "I'm glad you finally noticed."

Was she wrong — or did Tony look slightly disapproving as he nodded his head and said, "I've noticed for some time now." Then he asked, "Do you have a date this Saturday night?"

"No," Maggie whispered.

"Want to go to the movies with me?" Tony asked.

"Yes," Maggie answered. She couldn't think of anything to add, so she said it again. "Yes."

Eleven

In a way, going out with Tony felt very natural. After all, she had gone to the movies with Tony many times before. At the same time that it felt ordinary, it also felt very exciting because she had never gone to the movies with Tony as his date. Even though Tony was as comfortable as an old shoe in some ways, it was very special to be sitting beside him with no one else around.

Maggie was very conscious of the feelings which seemed to snap and crackle between them every time Tony reached over to take some of the popcorn she held in her hands. She hoped when they finished eating popcorn that he would hold her hand or put his arm around her shoulder. He didn't. He seemed engrossed in the movie. By the time the second feature began, Maggie had pretty well accepted the fact that whatever _she_ thought was between them, Tony didn't seem to be feeling the same way. As far as Maggie could see, there was nothing very exciting for him about being alone with her.

By the time the second feature was about half-way through, Maggie was feeling very alone. Why had she thought that one kiss would change everything? Tony was still thinking of her as his little sister. She was the same Maggie Matthews who had tagged along behind him for so many years. Why should she suddenly turn into someone who was different? She would always be the girl next door to him — plain old Maggie Matthews.

As she was thinking all these grumpy thoughts, she was watching a comedy on the screen. Maggie watched the heroine sweep through a large office, nodding to the right and to the left, then walk into her grand executive suite and sit behind the desk. She was so cool and poised. Maggie sighed a deep sigh and told herself it was silly to compare herself to an actress in a movie. Of course she could never be that casual or sophisticated. Ordinary people weren't, and she was ordinary.

As she was thinking all of these dark thoughts, Tony interrupted her by asking, "Do you want some more popcorn?"

Maggie shook her head no, thinking that the last thing she needed was to get any fatter. Comparing herself to the actress on the screen had made her feel very frumpy. She promised herself that she would stop doing that sort of thing. It would be better if she could learn not to compare herself to anyone, she decided — not even Denise. At the thought of Denise, she glanced up and saw Tony getting up from his chair. He walked out to the lobby of the theater to get a second box of popcorn. Was Tony wishing that he were with Denise tonight? Was he already sorry he had invited Maggie to go with him to see the movie? He seemed more withdrawn and more unfriendly than she had ever seen him. Usually Tony had a joke, or at least a smile for her, but this evening, he had picked her up and taken her to the movies without saying much of anything.

She began to wish that the movie would be over so she could go back to her house and be alone again. Going out with Tony wasn't as great as she had always dreamed it would be. Somehow, being around Tony made her feel worse about herself. It seemed to Maggie that she was really turning into a boring person. All she ever did was worry about how she looked or who she was. Why had she ever wanted to grow up? When she was ten, she had thought that growing up would make her something like the sleek and sophisticated actress on the screen, but now that she truly was growing up, life wasn't a bit easier. If anything, it was harder than she had imagined.

Where was Tony? Why was it taking him so long to get a box of popcorn? Maggie squirmed in her seat and turned around just in time to see Tony walking down the aisle of the theater with Denise. Maggie's heart dropped into her stomach.

She should have known. Her first and only date with Tony was spoiled now. She knew he would have preferred to be out with Denise this evening.

Tony slipped into the seat beside Maggie as though nothing was unusual or out of the ordinary. He offered popcorn to Maggie two or three times. She refused, staring straight ahead at the screen, without even looking at Tony. He ate the popcorn by himself and seemed to be enjoying the movie, laughing at all the funny lines. Maggie knew for certain that he was just putting on a good act. He wasn't really having a good time.

She didn't bother to try to laugh when she was expected to. It was too much trouble. When the movie was over, Tony asked, "You didn't like it much, did you?"

"Oh, I thought it was good enough," Maggie said.

"But not as sophisticated as some of the old Carole Lombard movies, huh?" Tony asked her.

Maggie was surprised that Tony even knew who Carole Lombard was. He usually didn't watch old movies. In fact, he usually made fun of her for watching them. She said, "I didn't know that you were a Carole Lombard fan."

Tony shrugged and made a slight face. "I've been trying to catch some of the older movies on television ever since I heard you and your friend talking about them. I thought it might be an interesting hobby."

"Do you like Carole Lombard?" Maggie asked.

Again, Tony made a face and said, "Not really, but I can see how you might get into old movies if you watched enough of them."

Maggie let the subject drop. It was clear Tony

didn't really have any interest in Carole Lombard or old movies or, for that matter, in Maggie herself. When he offered to buy her a piece of pizza, she said, "You don't have to if you're tired, Tony."

She waited for him to make an excuse and take her home, but he didn't. Instead, he said, "I'm not tired, if you're not. I saw Denise and she said a lot of the kids were going to the Pizza Palace."

Again Maggie's hopes sank as she realized that Tony's invitation to the Pizza Palace would include a lot of people. Worst of all, it would include Denise. She wanted to say that she would prefer not to go, but she didn't. Instead, she nodded her head in agreement. Whether she had a romance with Tony or not, she would have to stay on good terms with him. He was her brother's best friend, and there was no way that she could break off the relationship or arrange to never see him again. Tony Angelo was in her life for once and for all, no matter how unhappy she might be about it.

Tony held her hand as they walked out of the theater and down the street to get into his car. She knew it didn't mean anything. Tony was a warm and friendly guy, and holding hands was as natural for him as smiling or laughing or joking.

In spite of all the warnings she gave herself, Maggie couldn't help but enjoy the warm, wonderful feelings that holding hands with Tony made her feel. A current of happiness ran through her palm and went straight to her heart.

As they walked, Maggie was happy. The fearful and sad things she had been saying to herself seemed to disappear. Tony was nice to be with. When she was out with Alan, she always felt she should be at attention, laughing, nodding, smiling, or listening to him. Tony was much easier to be with because he was a quiet, happy person. With Tony she could just be herself.

He helped Maggie into the car and went around to his own side. When he got in, he turned to her and said seriously, "Look, Maggie, you don't have to go with me if you don't want to. I mean, if you're bored, that's okay. I can take you home."

Again, Maggie's stomach seemed to do a flip-flop. Her first thought was, *He's trying to get rid of me.* She wondered how she could have such extraordinary changes of emotions with a person who made her happy. Why was it that the least little thing that Tony said to her made her do emotional somersaults? She wished that she could always feel as peaceful and comfortable as she had just a moment ago when they were walking down the street.

She turned slightly toward him and said in a soft, timid voice, "Tony, if you don't want to take me for pizza, it's okay. I'll understand."

"And if you don't want to go, that's okay," Tony responded quickly. "I'll understand."

They both sat silently, waiting for the other one to say something. Maggie watched Tony in the darkness that was softly lit by a golden street lamp behind his head, feeling a warm flush of love wash over her. She said aloud, "You look so handsome in that half-light." There, it was out. She'd told him honestly what she thought!

143

Tony laughed a soft, deep-throated laugh that Maggie had never heard before. He said in a low, sweet voice, "That's funny, Margaret. I was thinking the same thing about you."

Maggie offered, "Maybe it's a magical light."

Tony nodded, bending slightly toward her. "Magical moonlight," he said.

Maggie shook her head quickly. "It's not moonlight; it's a street lamp. There isn't any moon tonight."

"There's always a moon where you are, Maggie," Tony said. "You bring moonlight wherever you go."

Maggie took a deep breath and her eyes opened wider. She said in a surprised voice, "Why, Tony, I had no idea you could say things like that. You sound absolutely romantic."

Tony's head moved quickly backward, and Maggie realized that he had been about to kiss her. Why had she ruined it? Why hadn't she just accepted the compliment? She wanted to tell him that she was sorry. There were many things she wanted to tell him.

Finally, after another long moment of silence, she said in a small, tentative voice, "I like it when you say romantic things, Tony. It makes me feel good, and I like it that you tell me I'm like moonlight. I didn't mean to hurt your feelings."

Tony shrugged. "I guess it does sound dumb coming from someone you've known all your life. It just doesn't do to try to be romantic when you've been around somone for as many years as we've been around each other, Maggie."

Maggie's spirits lifted at what Tony was saying. Whatever it meant, she was going to take a risk and tell him how she felt about him. She wasn't going to let him go by default.

She said, "It's different dating someone you've been around all your life, but it doesn't make it less romantic. As far as I'm concerned, you're a very romantic guy. I like you a lot better than the hero in that movie we just saw."

Tony's face seemed to brighten, and he turned back to her. He asked, "Really, Maggie? Do you mean that?"

She nodded her head. Was it possible that Tony could sometimes be insecure? Funny how she'd always been so busy thinking about covering up her own fears that it had never even occurred to her that he might have some of his own.

"You remind me a lot of the heroine in the movie," Tony said. "You look a little like her, too."

Maggie was startled at his comment. She was sure that he was wrong. She didn't look a thing like the woman in the movie. But this time she kept her mouth shut, saying only, "Thank you."

Tony reached out and touched her cheek, saying, "You both have high cheekbones and bright eyes. You're really very beautiful, Maggie. I guess you have been for a long time, haven't you?"

Maggie was so busy enjoying the touch of Tony's hand on her cheek that she didn't answer. She turned her head slightly and let her cheek lie in the palm of his hand, softly kissing his fingers with her lips. The touch of his skin, the warmth of his palm against her cheek, the feel of his hand against her lips, was lovely.

He whispered in her ear, "Yes. You are very beautiful, Maggie, and I like being with you a lot." On the final words, "a lot," his lips touched her ear and then trailed softly across her cheek, dropping down onto her lips for a full and complete kiss.

Just as she had the last time, Maggie found herself falling into a timeless feeling as she kissed Tony. He was so very special and so very dear to her.

Kissing Tony was a little like floating through space. There was a weightless, soft, mellow quality to the kiss. He drew away and caught his breath, taking her face in his two hands, spreading his hands across her cheeks, and letting his thumbs drop to the corners of her mouth. He said in a rough, deep voice, "My beautiful Maggie. Maggie of the Moonlight."

Then he dropped his hands, shook his head slightly, and tried to laugh to cover up the deepness of his feelings. He said in a more normal voice, "I guess I watched enough of those old movies to learn how to really ham it up, didn't I?"

But Maggie was so caught up in the moment and in the mood created by his caresses, she didn't immediately fall into his lighter mood. She said, breathing deeply, "I think you're wonderful, Tony. I have always thought you were wonderful."

Tony looked surprised. "Really?" he asked.

Maggie nodded her head yes.

146

He let out a deep sigh and said, "Well, that's something for the books. I thought that after you started dating that college boy, you'd be bored running around with a high school kid like me."

"I'm not interested in Alan," Maggie said. "I've never been. You're the only one I've ever been interested in, Tony."

Again, he asked, "Really?"

"Yes, really, but you always seemed interested in everyone but me. I mean, you have been dating Denise, you know."

"I only went out with Denise three times," Tony said quickly.

"And I only went out with Alan once," Maggie reminded him.

They both laughed at that. It was clear that some agreement had been reached between them. The laughter seemed as happy and warm as the kisses. Maggie leaned back against the back of the car and looked out at the blackness, lightened by street lamps as they drove toward the Pizza Palace.

She had never in her life been as completely happy as she was at that moment. *If only*, she told herself, *if only it lasts.*

Twelve

When Maggie and Tony walked into the Pizza Palace, Denise waved and called. Then she raised herself halfway out of her chair, and called again, "Tony, Tony," to make sure that they would see them.

Maggie felt a sharp intake of breath and realized that she was still a little jealous. Denise made her nervous, though she knew Tony was as honest as anyone could be. But just because Tony thought he was more interested in her than in Denise didn't mean it was necessarily true. Maybe Tony didn't know his own mind. Lots of boys didn't.

Even as she was thinking all these negative thoughts, Maggie was telling herself that it simply wasn't true. Tony did know his own mind. The farthest thing from anything she could imagine was Tony deliberately deceiving her.

He squeezed her hand and she smiled at him. Perhaps he knew that she was a little nervous about ending their date by being with Denise and the other kids. But even if she was nervous, she was determined to be a good sport about it. She realized she was making herself miserable for no good reason. Tony had said he thought she was wonderful. What more could she ask for? *Nothing*, Maggie told herself — *absolutely nothing at all*.

She smiled cheerfully at Denise and her date, Rod. The other couple were Jeffrey and Sharon. Since she knew all of the kids there, she felt reasonably comfortable and was able to join in their conversation about the coming ski season with easy enthusiasm. As they talked, Tony said, "Maggie and I might go up to Stowe Mountain this winter."

Denise raised an eyebrow and asked in a surprised voice, "Alone?"

Tony laughed at the idea, saying with easy familiarity, "If you knew Maggie's folks you wouldn't even ask. No, the whole Matthews family is talking about taking a week's vacation at Stowe."

Denise raised an eyebrow and said teasingly, "And you're just part of the family?"

Tony nodded his head cheerfully and smiled at Maggie as he winked. Then he replied to Denise, "That's right, just one big happy family. Maggie's just like a sister to me." The idea seemed to strike him as very funny. He rolled back his head and laughed at the idea.

Maggie was happy to see Tony taking it so well, and she found his laughter infectious. Soon the two of them were laughing so hard that the other kids at the table joined in.

Soon after that, Maggie yawned and said to Tony, "I think I'd like to go home now, if that's all right with you."

Tony was on his feet instantly and said, "Your wish is my command."

Denise smiled. "Tony, how did you learn to talk like that?"

Tony smiled, too, and said, "Oh, Maggie's an old movie fan, so I've been watching, too. I wanted to see what it was about Clark Gable that impressed her so. From now on, I'm going to be just like him." Then he put on a mock-questioning face and, turning to Maggie, said in a very cultured voice, "Or would you prefer Fred Astaire?"

Maggie laughed and answered, "I prefer variety. One day I think I'm Ginger Rogers and the next day I feel just like Bette Davis. It's a wonderful way to live."

Tony linked his arm through hers and turned to the group, clicking his heels and bowing from the waist as he said, "And I think that it's a wonderful way to live as well. Every day a new and more dashing personality." With that, he twirled an imaginary mustache and asked hopefully, "Do I remind you all of Errol Flynn?"

Maggie and he were laughing as they left the restaurant.

All the way home from the Pizza Palace, Tony tried out different imitations of old movie stars on Maggie. By the time they got to the front door, she was laughing much longer and much louder than she'd done in the movie.

Tony's mood seemed to change rapidly as he parked the car and turned off the ignition key. He became himself again, saying quietly, "I'm sorry I suggested we go out with those guys, Maggie. I'd rather have been alone with you."

Maggie shrugged and said, "Tony, I had a good time. I had a wonderful evening. Honest, I did."

"Me, too," Tony said, and then he reached over and pulled Maggie close to him, kissing her firmly and enthusiastically. This kiss was different from any of the others because it was a stronger, more possessive kiss. There was not the element of surprise, and it seemed more as though Tony were claiming her as his girlfriend.

Maggie felt comfortable in his arms. She responded as quickly as before. When they finally pulled apart, she whispered in a soft voice, "I've got to go in now, Tony, or my folks will be worried. It really was a wonderful evening."

She waited for a moment, hoping that Tony would ask her out again. When he didn't, she opened the car door and walked toward the house alone. Some of the old feelings of *Does he love me? Doesn't he love me?* returned. She was disappointed he hadn't walked her to the door. Weren't boys supposed to walk their girlfriends to the door? Why hadn't he?

Even as she was thinking these things, she shook her head and reminded herself that her evening with Tony had turned out much, much better than she had expected. She had spent the first half of the evening wondering if he even liked her, making herself miserable for no good reason. Now she was not going to turn this wonderful date around and make herself miserable again. She was going to grab this happiness and hug it close to her. This was the best date that she had ever been on with the best boy that she had ever dated. She was not going to let a little thing like not being walked to the front door ruin it for her. She knew she had a talent for turning small things into big productions, and she wasn't going to do that anymore.

She was surprised when she went into the house to find everyone still up. She asked, "How come you're all here?"

Bruce, who was popping popcorn, laughed and said, "I decided to come home from college this weekend after all. I just got in, so the folks stayed up. Bob just got in from a date."

Maggie looked around the kitchen table. She laughed and said, "We look like one of those families on TV commercials. Everyone's so happy and homey and good-looking."

"You're the prettiest of all," Mrs. Matthews said. "You look absolutely radiant. Did you have a good time?"

"Oh, yes," Maggie said. "It was a wonderful evening!"

Bruce asked, "Got a new fellow, Maggie?"

Maggie blushed and said, "Not exactly new. I went out with Tony tonight."

Bruce nodded as though that was the most natural thing in the world and went on popping the corn. He said, "Well, your old fellow sent you a present. It's over there." Bruce pointed to the kitchen cabinet, where his suitcase sat on the floor. For the first time, Maggie saw the large box of chocolates.

She went over and picked up the chocolates and said, "It's a five-pound box. He must have spent a fortune."

Bruce laughed and said, "Nothing's too good for my sister."

Maggie asked, "You didn't buy these, did you?"

Bruce said, "Of course not. They're from Alan. There's a note."

Maggie opened the box of chocolates and passed it around the table. Her mother took a chocolate and said, "You'd better open the note, Maggie."

Maggie didn't really feel like opening a note from Alan at this moment. Her head was too full of Tony. Wasn't it funny the way Tony had been afraid he couldn't compete with Alan, when all the time, Alan was no competition at all? "I'll read it tomorrow."

"That poor boy," Mrs. Matthews sighed as she took another chocolate. "I think you should read his note before I finish the box of candy. It doesn't seem fair somehow."

Reluctantly, Maggie slit open the envelope and a card with a picture of Rita Hayworth fell out onto the table. Maggie picked up the card and looked at the old black-and-white photo of the 1940's film star, whose red hair fluffed out in a long, glamorous pageboy. She smiled at the card and opened it to find that there was a poem inside. The poem read, "To Margaret, my love:

Each night I dream of thee,
You are my star, my love,
You are my manifest destiny,
Of thee I sing my song of sorrow,
Blinded bright, I hope for tomorrow.
Give me a sign, my sweet siren.
My heart, my soul forever yours.

Love,

Alan"

Maggie read it through aloud. She didn't know whether to laugh or to cry. The poem was so bad and so silly. She hoped that he had intended it as a joke, but somehow she had the feeling that he meant every word of it.

There was a silence around the Matthewses' table, and then Tony's voice said clearly, "He should have finished the poem. The last two lines don't rhyme. It should have been, Give me a sign, my sweet siren. If you don't answer by tomorrow, I'm going to give up tryin'."

Maggie was upset knowing that Tony had heard Alan's poem. She wheeled around and said, "How did you get in here?"

Tony shrugged and grinned at her as he leaned over and picked up a piece of chocolate from the box. He said, "I didn't want to walk you up to the front door and then not come in myself after I'd kissed you good night. So I just decided to wait a minute and come in the back way like I usually do."

"That's not fair," Maggie cried. "You sneaked up on me."

"I always sneak up on you," Tony pointed out

practically. "I hope you're not mad. Say you're not mad, Maggie."

He looked genuinely worried, and Maggie knew she couldn't stay mad at him for even a minute. She lifted the box of chocolates and said, "Try these. I think they're chocolate-covered butterfingers. I'm not mad, I guess, but it seems weird."

Tony nodded companionably and sat down at the table with Mr. and Mrs. Matthews. He said, "It *is* weird having a girlfriend who's also part of your adopted family. We're going to have to work out some new rules, I guess. Maybe I could kiss you good night at the front door and then come around the back of the house. Then I could kiss you good night again."

Everyone laughed except Maggie, who blushed a furious color of scarlet. She said in a most exasperated voice, "If I'd thought you were going to come in here and make fun of me, I never would have let you kiss me good night the first time."

"How about the second time?" Bruce said as he put the popcorn on the table.

Maggie looked around the ring of laughing faces and decided it was no use being angry. If she was going to date her brother's best friend, she would have to expect a certain amount of kidding. She joined in the laughter and then quickly tried to change the subject by asking, "Do you think we could all go to Stowe Mountain this winter? I'd love a week of skiing vacation. Do you think we will be able to do that?"

"We might be able to," Mrs. Matthews agreed

amicably. "At least, your father and I hope we'll be able to. It would be fun." Then her face changed and she said, "Maggie, you've got to be firmer with Alan. You've got to tell him you're really not interested in him at all. I don't like the idea of everyone laughing at that poor young man. You mustn't be the sort of woman who leads men on."

Maggie nodded her head and said, "I'll call him tomorrow, Mother, and I'll be very firm. I'll explain it all to him as carefully as I can."

As she made this promise, Tony grabbed her hand under the table and squeezed it tightly. Then he said, "Make it an early morning call. I thought maybe you and I could go on a bike ride tomorrow afternoon. That is, if you want to go for a bike ride. We could go down to the Bartlett Orchards maybe and pick apples. Would you like that?"

"I'd like that," Maggie answered.

"And then next weekend I thought we might spend some time going over our skis, getting them ready. What do you think about that?"

"I think that's a wonderful idea," Maggie answered. She looked at Tony. "This is going to be the very best winter of my whole life. I'm sure it is."